Addicted to My Thug

Ari &

Miss Jenesequa

Remember....
You haven't read 'til you've read #Royalty
Check us out at
www.royaltypublishinghouse.com
Royalty drops #dopebooks

© 2015 Ari & Miss Jenesequa
Published by Royalty Publishing House
http://www.royaltypublishinghouse.com/

ALL RIGHTS RESERVED.

Contains explicit language & adult themes suitable for ages 16+

Books by Ari:

- *I'll Ride For My Thug 1*
- *I'll Ride For My Thug 2*
- *I'll Ride For My Thug 3*
- *Love, Betrayal & Dirty Money: A Hood Romance*
- *Addicted To My Thug*

Books By Miss Jenesequa:

- *Lustful Desires: Secrets, Sex & Lies*
- *Sex Ain't Better Than Love 1*
- *Sex Ain't Better Than Love 2*
- *Luvin' Your Man: Tales Of A Side Chick*
- *Down For My Baller 1*
- *Down For My Baller 2*
- *Bad For My Thug 1*
- *Bad For My Thug 2*
- *Addicted To My Thug*

~ A Note From Ari:

Amazing is the only word I can use to describe this feeling. Our novel is finally complete and we had so much fun doing it. My Royalty bestie Jenn, made this experience a memorable one, bringing so much creativity to the table. Both of our talents and positivity combined, made us a force to be reckoned with. Jenn, your beautiful personality and outgoing spirit brought so much joy to my heart. Not to mention your kick ass attitude that made me feel like together we could face the world and definitely leave our mark...

Thank you for being so understanding and working together with me to create the perfect balance within our novel. You are truly an amazing author and an inspiration to me. You helped me to step into a new world of writing and helped me tap into my inner freak! For that I'm forever grateful, and never change one bit. I love you to death just way you are because you're so real and true to who you are before anything else.

A big thank you goes to you Porscha Sterling for always being so supportive and pushing us to always give it our all. You saw greatness in me and took a chance with placing me under Royalty so that I could pursue my dreams. It's because of you that I have been able to find a lifelong friend and have the pleasure of meeting such a wonderful gal like Jenn.

Thank you all for purchasing our novel and believing us. I hope you enjoy it as much as we enjoyed writing it. Don't forget to leave a review because we'd love to hear your thoughts.

~ A Note From Miss Jen:

Wow... We finally did it. My royalty bestie and I decided months ago that we were going to change the game and bring our powers together in one book. This is that book. And to know that we've completed our first book together, truly brings happiness and love to my heart. Ari, you truly are the real MVP for being so real and kind to me. I love you, girl, you're definitely my favorite Royalty author and the realist I've come across. Don't you ever change girl! Keep doing and being you.

I just want to thank Ari for being so determined and patient with me. I know being a mother gets tough sometimes and you're constantly busy, but even through it all, Ari still went H.A.M on our masterpiece and continued to deliver nothing but pure talent.

I also want to thank Porscha Sterling. If it wasn't for her, creating Royalty and putting me in Royalty I wouldn't even know who Ari is. She's the true MVP. She was also extremely excited to read our collab and wouldn't stop squealing with delight every time she heard about it.

To Bad For My Thug Fans: I told you guys that Marquise's book was coming. Now here it is!

Thank you to everyone who has purchased this book and is now reading it. I hope you enjoy it, just as much as I enjoyed writing it. Ari and I worked our butts off writing this, so please don't hesitate to tell us what you think about it by leaving a review on Amazon.

PROLOGUE ~ ADDICTED TO HIM

Have you ever had the one thing... That one thing that you can't seem to get enough of?

Well that's exactly what happened to I, Naomi Evans, when I couldn't get enough of... *Him.* My addiction, my drug, my fiend. He was the one that managed to charm me, seduce me and fuck the living daylights out of me, making me always want him and come running straight back for more.

"You the baddest chick I ever been wit', " he said to me.

I don't know how he managed to do it so fast... Maybe it was that handsome face, that undeniable swag, that cocky attitude or maybe it was... The D.

"I think I'm fallin' for yo' freaky ass ma'," he whispered *passionately.*

Whatever it was... He's won. He's succeeded. He's made me fall in love with my addiction for him. I should have left him alone. I should have never given him a minute of my time. I was happy... right? Married to the man of my dreams, with our two wonderful kids. I was happy.

"I don't care if you busy tonight... I want you, completely naked, in my bed," he ordered over the phone. *"I ain't takin' no for an answer. Don't make me come find yo' ass."*

But he came along and switched up everything I thought I was fine with. Turns out I wasn't fine. I needed something more. He provided me with that and more, every single night. Whether it was in his car, in my car, at his crib, in a hotel, or even at work... He gave me that and more, and I loved every single fucking bit of it.

"What... You thought I was done fuckin' wit'chu?" He questioned *firmly. "Nah baby... I'm just gettin' fuckin' started with yo' sexy ass. Ain't no way I'm lettin' that bomb ass pussy of yours go."*

Who is this *he,* you ask? Well ask no more. You'll get to find out every single bit of my addiction. Just sit back and enjoy the ride.

"Stop fightin' this shit girl... You know you wan' me, and I want you," he stated. *"I'm the only one who fucks that pussy right."*

I promise it'll leave you wanting more... The same way he left me wanting him, every day.

CHAPTER 1 ~ ONE CLASSY BITCH

Naomi smiled as the rays of sun kissed her caramel skin while her class played outside during recess. Her naturally long curly hair swarmed around her, as a gentle breeze came her way. She found pure joy in moments like these where the children could be just that—children. She had dreamed of being a teacher from a small child and couldn't imagine being anything else. Their little smiles and pure excitement while learning, truly warmed her heart. She took pride in the fact that she had a lot to do with that and vowed to always do her best.

"My goodness I'll be glad when this day is over," Erin smiled as she stood next to Naomi.

"What, don't tell me you're ready for our little monsters to leave just yet," Naomi chuckled.

"Don't get me wrong, I love these munchkins just as much as you do. But, I'm in dire need of some girl time. Do you know how long it's been since I had some dick?" Erin whispered.

"Oh my god, Erin! Don't start girl," Naomi laughed lightly.

"Girl, I am serious. I'm ready to trade in the finger paint for some cocktails! You are still coming, right?" Erin questioned.

Naomi mentally kicked herself as she remembered that she promised her best friend that she would go out with her and a few others for drinks. It had been months since they had hung out together and after some coaching, she had relented. She rarely ever did anything with her best friend these days. Between her husband and children, she rarely had time to herself. Naomi frowned as she chewed her bottom lip. Was she really willing to go out tonight?

"I know that look Naomi. Don't you even think about trying to get out of it. Come on girl; it's just for a few hours, I promise," Erin pleaded.

"Come on Erin. I know I promised, but why do we have to go to a club? Can't we watch Netflix and pop open a bottle of wine," Naomi said as a pout formed upon her lips.

"No we cannot! Naomi, when is the last time you put on a dress and some makeup? Besides, you know I've been dying to go to that new spot downtown. I heard that there are some fine ass men all up and through there," Erin declared.

"Girl you are a trip. You just want to be a little thot," Naomi laughed as she swatted Erin's arm.

"Sure do! I'm single and ain't nothing wrong with a little eye candy that may turn into some desert hunny!" Erin smiled.

"You are sick!" Naomi chuckled.

"Not sick just horny as hell. I need some dick. A big one too," Erin whispered as they both broke out into uncontrollable laughter.

"Okay, I'll be there. Text me the details and I'll meet you," Naomi agreed.

Erin grinned like the Cheshire cat as she embraced her best friend. Naomi giggled at her excitement. She had to admit that she was in dire need of some girl time herself, but she always felt somewhat out of place in a club. She preferred a more laid back environment where she could be herself. She was married, after all, to a wonderful man and had two beautiful children at home. In her mind, there wasn't a damn thing in any club that she would ever need because she loved her man.

"Ms. Evan's class, please line up!" Naomi yelled as she attempted to gather her little ones. She patiently waited as the stragglers took their sweet time moving towards the line, while glancing at the time on her watch.

"Hands folded in front of you guys and it's time for our what?" Naomi asked.

"Our inside voices!" the children recited.

"That's right my little superstars! Now let's go inside and get our things," Naomi instructed as she turned to walk towards her class. She giggled at Erin who was currently removing wood chips from one of her student's mouth. She turned to glance at her class who was right behind her, as they entered the building and made their way to their classroom. Once they were inside, the children began to gather their things as she walked around and handed out stickers to each child.

"Okay everyone, make sure we grab all of our things quietly," Naomi instructed as she glanced in the direction of two of her students who were currently racing to see who could get done first.

"Alright everyone, let's line up," Naomi said just as the bell rang. She escorted everyone into the hallway after ensuring that all of her students were accounted for. She patiently waited as each parent gathered their children so that she could go home and prepare for the night's festivities.

***

"Now I got love all over me… Baby you touched every part of me… Oh," Naomi sang along to Monica as she pulled her Nissan Altima into her driveway, parking beside her husband's truck. She had stopped off at the mall on her way home so that she could grab something to wear. God knows she didn't have a single thing in her closet that would be considered to be club attire. She had managed to find a dress from Wet Seal that she was convinced would be perfect for the night. She turned off the ignition before grabbing her bags and closing the door behind her with her hip. She hit the alarm as she struggled to hold on to her purse upon entering her home. She was quickly greeted at the door by her two children.

"Mommy! Mommy!" Josie and Christopher yelled as they wrapped their little arms around her legs. "We missed you!"

"Well hello my little love bugs! Mommy missed you too!" she cooed as her husband, Tyree entered the room.

"Hey baby. Looks like you got your hands full there," he said as he grabbed her bags and placed a gentle kiss on her lips.

Naomi smiled as she looked into his eyes before bending down to kiss both of her kids on the forehead.

"Daddy missed you, too," Tyree smiled as he set her bags down on the couch in the living room.

"I missed you too, sweetie," Naomi said as she walked towards him and embraced him in a loving hug.

"Daddy's playing hide and seek with us mommy!" Josie admitted.

"Oh he is? Well you'd better go hide then before he finds you," Naomi said.

"One... Two... Three..." Tyree happily recited as the children both took off running towards their hiding place.

Naomi grabbed her purse just as Tyree reached for her bags and began following her upstairs towards their bedroom. "How was your day, baby?" Tyree asked.

"It went well, honey. My little superstars were anxious for the weekend as usual," Naomi admitted as she set her purse on the dresser and kicked off her shoes.

"Yea', I bet. I can remember that feeling when I was a kid," Tyree admitted while placing her bags on the bed.

"How was your day, baby?" Naomi asked while planting another kiss on his lips. She had missed her man all day and now that she was in his presence – Naomi felt happy.

"It was good for the most part until Christopher decided to glue some pictures to the wall," Tyree stated with a light chuckle.

"That boy knows he can come up with some stuff! What are we going to do with him?" Naomi laughed.

"Who you asking? I don't know and you know he gets that type of stuff from you," Tyree chuckled, teasing his wife playfully.

"Yea' right! You know that's all you," Naomi responded.

"What's all this? You goin' somewhere?" Tyree asked while nosily peeking inside one of her bags.

Naomi turned towards Tyree and replied with a reluctant head nod. "Uh yea. Erin invited me out for girl's night."

Tyree firmly folded his arms over his chest and responded, "Well, when were you going to ask me? I mean, how do you know I didn't have something planned for us?"

Naomi turned towards him with a confused expression. "I'm sorry baby, it totally slipped my mind and I promised her about a week ago," she explained. It had never really crossed her mind that Tyree would have a problem with her going out considering she never did. What was wrong with just one night away from him?

"Baby, I really wanted to just spend some quality time with you. It's not like we have many opportunities to do that considering we have the kids all the time," Tyree admitted truthfully.

"I understand baby and I apologize, but I can't just back out at the last minute. I promised her and besides, it's not like I go out all the time. Why are you trippin'?" Naomi questioned.

"Naomi, I'm not trippin; I'm your husband. You and Erin can hang out some other time. The kids are going to my mother's house tonight and I want to spend some time with you," Tyree demanded.

"Tyree, why are you raising your voice? I'm not going to go back and forth with you about this, okay? Just call your mother and ask if she can keep them tomorrow instead. I promise it will be just you and me," Naomi explained simply.

"Daddy, are you going to come find us?" Christopher suddenly yelled as Tyree stood in the middle of the room.

"Ready or not, here I come," Tyree yelled as he turned to exit the room.

Naomi reached out and gently placed a hand on his arm. "Baby, don't be mad at me. It's only for a few hours," she said.

"Yeah, whatever," Tyree said, shrugging her hand off as he exited the room while shaking his head.

Naomi flopped down on the bed and exhaled as she stared at the ceiling. If she had known this would be such a big deal, she would never have agreed. Part of her felt bad because she knew how exhausting being at home with the kids all day must be for her husband. He had been experiencing some hardships with finding a job and opted for staying home with the children because it worked better for their family.

What he didn't understand was that balancing a full-time job, being a wife, and mother was exhausting for her too. She felt he was being unreasonable and for that very reason, she was going out with her friend. She turned towards her bag and began to lay out her clothes for the night. She was going to make sure that she enjoyed herself despite everything she had going on. She walked to her jewelry box and began selecting pieces that would complement her dress. She then began looking for the perfect matching panty and bra set. She decided to run herself some bath water for some much needed pampering before her night out.

"As Erin would say, you only live once," Naomi said to herself and then entered the bathroom, closing the door behind her.

***

"And where the hell do you think you're going dressed like that?" Tyree questioned her rudely, looking at her up and down.

Naomi thought she looked good. More than good. She looked like a woman going out to the club should look – classy as fuck. She was one classy bitch and she knew it too. She ignored his question and continued staring at her beautiful image in the reflection in front of her. Clad in a knee high, tight, low-neck revealing baby pink dress with a lace design at the front, Naomi smiled at herself happily.

"Are you not listening to me Naomi? You're not leaving the house dressed like that," Tyree snapped. "You better change or somethin'. Wear something longer and put on a damn coat."

"I'm going to do whatever the fuck I want Tyree, and what I want is to go out to the club, dressed exactly how I want. Okay?" She looked at him with an arched brow, a strong look of determination now plastered upon her pretty face. He had been annoying her ever since he had popped up in the doorway and began complaining about her outfit.

"Naomi... I ain't gon' let you leave the house like this. You ca-"

"You're not the owner of my body, Tyree," she barked. "This is what I've decided to wear to the club and this is how I'm leaving the house."

"Are you serious?"

"Dead serious," she said.

And once he no longer seemed bothered to reply, Naomi began continuing her finishing touches to her makeup, before adding, "Don't bother waiting up for me either. I'll be home when I want to be home. And it won't be the time you want me to be."

"So you're basically acting like a hoe tonight, right?" he asked her, his arms crossed across his chest while he leaned in their bedroom doorway, still watching her.

"You calling your wife a hoe?"

"No," he stated through gritted teeth. "I'm asking my wife if she's acting like a hoe tonight, because it sure seems like it."

"Well if I'm acting like a hoe, then you should leave me to it, right?"

"If that's what you want."

"That's what I want. Now leave me the fuck alone."

The tension between Naomi and Tyree had grown from 0 to 100 real quick. He wanted to shake some sense into her and find out what had come over her, whereas she wanted to give him a slap for always trying to be so damn controlling. She was her own woman and she was going to start acting like it more often. She couldn't breathe with him always trying to make her do things his way. Today she did things her way. Today would be the night of many nights living it up with her girlfriend.

Fuck Mr. Tyree Evans.

CHAPTER 2 ~ SEXY STRANGER

Somebody come get her, she's dancin' like a stripper… Somebody come get her, she's dancin' like a stripper. Somebody come tip her, she's dancin' like a stripper.

"I'm so glad you came out tonight Naomi," Erin said loudly above the booming music. "All the other girls bailed out on us."

"Oh really? Did they say why exactly?" Naomi queried curiously before taking a small sip of her martini.

"Nah," Erin stated with a head shake. "But they're boring as hell anyway, all I need is you. You're the only who knows how to really have fun!"

Naomi couldn't help but chuckle at her best friend's words. She wasn't exactly sure if she was the only who knew how to have fun, but she definitely knew how to have a good time. And tonight she was going to make sure that she had the time of her life.

Ten minutes later, after drinking some more of their drinks and getting a good vibe of the club they were at, Erin and Naomi finally made it to the dance floor. They both began to move and grind their hips to the upbeat music, letting the euphoric high from the music overcome them.

Naomi danced like she had never danced before. This was a way for her to get rid of all the stress and anger she had been feeling before coming to the club tonight. Tyree had given her a hard time for no reason. All she wanted to do was let her hair down one night with her girl. What was the harm in that?

The music sounded through her ears beautifully and began to take her to a high that she had missed feeling these past few months. For the first time in what seemed like forever, Naomi felt free.

The more she danced, the more attention she began to draw to herself. People on the dance floor were beginning to notice her seductive moves and a few males had moved closer, in hopes of getting a dance with her.

One man in particular couldn't take his eyes off her. She had managed to grab his attention the minute she arrived in his club. And now seeing her move those curvy hips and shake that ass with her girlfriend, made Marquise heat up with a sudden burning desire for her.

He hadn't been having a good day. Not at all. After finding out that one of his trap houses had been attacked by a rival gang/arch enemy, Marquise had been in a bad mood all night. But seeing this beauty move on the dance floor had managed to wash away all his bad vibes.

When their eyes met, Marquise shot her a sexy smile before biting his lips at her. *Fuck, she's beautiful.*

She was caramel, with straight, long brown hair that passed her shoulders and stopped just under her breasts. Her pretty brown eyes had a story behind them. A story that intrigued Marquise the more he stared at her. She had a body on her too. A nice, curvy and thick in all the right places body. Her tits were round and perky and from all that dancing she had been doing, he had already seen a great view of her ass.

Naomi couldn't believe this guy was now staring at her. She had felt someone in particular watching her in the crowd but now looking at the VIP booth and seeing him sitting comfortable on a red loveseat with two models all up on him but his hazel eyes on her only, had her low key gassed.

He was handsome. Very handsome indeed. Staring into his hazel eyes was nice and with how fine he was, with those cute dimples, straight white teeth, plump kissable lips, smooth milk chocolate skin, low fade hair cut with a freshly trimmed goatee that lined up perfectly against his lips - she was really enjoying looking at him.

And with the way that black tailored suit fit him so well, and the way that iced out silver watch sparkled in the dimly lit light - Naomi had to admit she was impressed.

"Gurl, I need to go to the restroom," Erin suddenly announced.

"Alright hun, let's go."

Following Erin to the restrooms made Naomi sadly break eye contact with the sexy stranger in the VIP section. As much as she wanted to stay and continue to stare at the fine man, making sure her friend got to the restrooms safely was now more important.

When finally arriving, Erin entered one of the restroom cubicles, leaving Naomi to stare at her pretty reflection. She still looked good and she knew that's why the sexy stranger had been paying her any mind, just like all the other dudes watching her.

She briefly thought about Tyree and how she didn't want to get home too late. Then she thought *fuck it. It's a Friday, I'm letting my hair down. End of. There's no harm in looking at a fine nigga.*

Erin finally came out the cubicle, washed her hands and was now ready to head back to the dance floor.

"See how many guys have come up to me already? I'm getting some dick tonight," she sang happily before opening the restroom door for them to exit.

Naomi laughed before commenting behind her, "You're something else Erin, I swear..." Naomi's words instantly trailed off once Erin who was walking in front of her, suddenly stopped.

Naomi looked up only to be greeted to the handsome face of the sexy stranger from the VIP section.

"Can I buy you beautiful ladies, a drink?"

Hearing his deep baritone and that sexy Atlanta accent of his, had Naomi's panties instantly getting wet. And seeing that wild look in his hazel eyes up close, was sure to drive her crazy with lust for him. His diamond stud earrings locked in each ear, only enchanted Naomi even more to see what he had to offer.

How could she resist a drink from this sexy stranger?

CHAPTER 3 ~ PURE SEDUCTION

Naomi bit down on her bottom lip while she eyed the gorgeous man standing in front of her.

"Sure, why not," Naomi replied as he plastered the sexiest grin ever on his face.

"Follow me," he said as he began to lead the way back out into the packed club. Naomi glanced at Erin who walked beside her as she mouthed the words *"He is fine as hell!"* Naomi chuckled as they stopped outside of the VIP section where he whispered something to the bouncer.

"Ladies," he said as he stepped aside and allowed them to enter the section first. They made their way to a sectional where they each took a seat before they were greeted by a server.

"What would you like to drink?" he asked.

"I'll have Henny straight," Erin declared happily.

"Cîroc with a splash of pineapple juice," Naomi stated. He smirked while making eye contact with Naomi. Naomi felt her heart rate accelerate while he undressed her with his eyes. Never had a man looked at her as if he wanted nothing more than to devour her, and Naomi found herself staring at him the same way.

Erin smiled as she glanced back and forth between the two of them. The tension was so thick in their section that anyone passing by could sense it. Naomi finally broke eye contact as their drinks were brought to them and placed on the table in front of them.

"Thank you," Naomi said gently as she reached for her drink.

"You're welcome," he said, just as a man approached him and tapped him on the shoulder before whispering something in his ear.

"Will you excuse me for a minute?" he asked.

"Sure," Erin responded as the sexy stranger excused himself and followed the man over to the bar.

Erin slid closer to her best friend and suddenly said, "Well it's obvious that he wants you, but what's surprising is that you want him too, huh?"

Naomi blushed as she turned towards Erin with a shocked expression on her face. "What? No! I mean he's cute and all, but I'm a married woman," she replied.

Erin chuckled as she waved her hand to dismiss Naomi's explanation. "Honey, even a blind man can see the sexual chemistry between you two. You're right, you are a married woman. But what's wrong with some conversation, dancing, drinks, and having a really good time?" she asked curiously before lifting her glass to her lips.

Naomi blew out a deep breath and said, "God that man is fine. Erin, you know usually I wouldn't entertain anyone at all, but it's something about him that I cannot resist."

"And with that being said girl, let your hair down and live a little. When is the last time you did you without having to take into consideration your husband and kids? Just for tonight you can be whoever you want to be," Erin exclaimed excitedly.

Naomi smiled at her best friend as they both took sips from their drinks.

"Now that we got that out of the way, that eye candy at the bar has had eyes on me since we walked in VIP. I'll leave you two so that you can get to know each other a bit better. Text me if you need me babe," Erin declared as she stood up while taking a sip from her drink and began walking in the direction of the bar.

Naomi nervously smoothed her hair and adjusted her dress. She now felt somewhat insecure, knowing that she was going to be all alone with the sexy stranger while Erin talked her way into someone's bed. She knew Erin was right and the fact that she had not had any time to herself was the exact reason that she was there.

As if he could sense her thinking of him, he made his way towards her taking a seat closer to her than before.

"What's your name gorgeous?" he asked.

Just for tonight you can be whoever you want to be girl, Naomi thought, remembering Erin's words as she stared at the sexiest lips she had ever laid eyes on.

"My name is Nicole," Naomi responded as she extended her hand.

"Nice to meet you, ma. I'm Marquise," he replied smoothly as he took her hand into his and bowed down to place a gentle kiss on it.

Naomi crossed her legs as she felt a sudden rush from the sensation of his soft warm lips upon her skin. His hand then roamed up her wrist and onto her arm, where he gently rubbed back and forth.

"I gotta be honest with you, shorty. I know you seen me starin' at you from across the room and I had to say somethin' to you. You so fuckin' bad and I just gotta have you," Marquise declared as his hand moved further up her arm and onto her shoulder. His straight forwardness was surprisingly turning her on.

Naomi stared into his eyes. "Well Marquise, how do you know I'm not taken?" she shyly asked.

"I don't, but what I do know is that any nigga that let you step out without havin' you on his arm gotta be out of his damn mind," he replied confidently.

Naomi smiled at his response while taking another sip of her drink. "What about you? I know there are tons of women who would love to be on your arm."

Marquise chuckled as he tossed the rest of his drink back. He gently tucked her hair behind her ear and leaned forward. "Shorty, ain't no woman on this earth been able to hold my attention with just one smile. Neva mind them other bitches cuz you already wiped them out of existence when you agreed to sit down and have a drink with me. You a good girl Nicole, and you tryna be bad for the night. Why not choose to be bad with me?" Marquise asked as his tongue found his way to her ear lobe.

Naomi bit down on her bottom lip as she briefly closed her eyes, while images of his hands all over her filled her head. The cold but soft feel of his tongue on her ear had her horniness increase from 0 to 100 real quick, and the thing that that shocked her the most was that this was a feeling she had yet to embrace in ages. *When was the last time you got really freaky, Naomi?*

"If you only knew the things I want to do to you. I swear I'll put some shit on you that you ain't never gon' forget baby," Marquise admitted seductively, as he continued to suck her ear lobe while gently placing her hand on his manhood which stood rock hard at her attention. "You feel this shit? You feel how hard you got me?"

Naomi couldn't think straight with him being so close to her. And once she could feel what she was doing to him, she swore she was in ecstasy. Not to mention this man was turning her on his ways that she could have never imagined. Naomi's eyes fluttered open to find that Erin was no longer at the bar talking to her desert for the night.

"Can I have you Nicole? Can I have your mind and body jus' for tonight?" Marquise questioned her lustfully.

Naomi turned in his direction just as Marquise did before letting him place a soft kiss on her lips. Fuck it. She wanted this man tonight. And she was just going to have him. She didn't know what it was about him, but he was one sexy motherfucker that she wanted inside her, all night. Her lips parted as she felt his tongue attempting to push its way through. She welcomed it as she softly sucked on his tongue and bottom lip, while her hand was still firmly gripping his manhood. His hands firmly gripped her soft round ass as she softly moaned into his mouth.

"Tell me something good ma," Marquise demanded pulling their lips apart with a soft smack.

"Yes... you can have me just for tonight," Naomi responded in a soft whisper, before she could change her lust-filled mind.

CHAPTER 4 ~ FREAKY GIRL

"Take all yo' clothes off," he ordered firmly. *"Now."*

She wasn't sure how it happened. All she knew was that it did. One minute he was sucking on her ear, the next minute he was leading her out the club, then she was in his Ferrari and before she knew it, she was fully naked on his burgundy king-sized bed, fit for a king only.

"This my pussy."

"It's yours baby."

"Say my name."

"Marquise, uh!"

"Marquise's pussy?"

"Marquise's pussy, baby, this is your pussy."

"You like this dick? You love it?"

"Yeah, agh! I love it. Fuck me baby."

How it happened? Naomi knew it had to be magic. There was no way that it couldn't have been. Because from the minute that he unlocked his apartment door and let her enter first, he was fast on her like a bee to a honey jar.

As soon as the door slammed shut behind her, Naomi felt her body being swirled around and before she knew it, she was up against the cold wall staring into nothing but his mesmerizing hazel eyes.

"I can't wait to be inside yo' pussy tonight," he whispered leaning into her soft neck to plant sweet kisses everywhere. Sniffing into her sweet scent had already began to send Marquise into an overdrive of sexual lust and desire for this hot lady.

His erotic kisses were already making Naomi's wetness flood into her panties. As much as she knew that what she was letting him do was wrong, she didn't want him to stop. He planted small, sweet kisses along her collarbone, up her neck, before gently moving his big hands down her back, down her ass, only to squeeze it tightly. A soft moan escaped Naomi's lips but no words telling him to stop sounded out.

Before she knew it, Marquise was on his knees, pulling down on her panties, letting them drop to her ankles, and lifting her dress up above her hips. "Yo' pussy so pretty ma'... And wet too? Fuck, how'd you get so wet for me?"

How'd she get so wet for him? Naomi wasn't sure she could answer such an explicit question even if she tried. "...Marquise, we sho-... Agh!" He was already beginning to tongue her down with that hot, talented tongue of his that she didn't know he had until now. She wanted to tell him to stop. She should have told him to stop. She was married. *Married.* But all that didn't mean shit now that his tongue was moving up and down the wet entrance of her pussy. He had started a burning fire within her and she knew that she needed to release it. She needed her sweet release tonight.

"Shit... Oh God..." Up one thick finger went, then the other followed blowing Naomi's mind completely insane. The only things she had ever had up there was Tyree's dick, her sex toys but certainly not Tyree's fingers and mouth. "Marquise!... Fuck."

"You love how that shit feels, right baby? Tell me," he said seductively, rubbing, stroking and pushing, completely blowing Naomi's mind further.

Naomi looked down into those lust-filled hazel eyes about to give him a simple head nod until his head disappeared deep between her legs, and that amazing tongue was already making her hot up with excitement again. From the very moment he licked, Naomi began speaking a different language that only he could understand. He was too good at this game and he knew it too.

Shit, he wasn't even expecting to eat this girl's pussy. But something about her from the very moment he laid eyes on her had him infatuated. She looked sweet and innocent and with the way she was reacting with her shaking and moaning, he knew she had never done this shit before. She had probably not even done most of the freaky shit he was planning to do with her tonight. It had been a month since Marquise had had some pussy. Being busy with his squad, making moves and making paper kept him one busy man. But not tonight. Tonight he got his way with Ms. Nicole.

Every lick, every swirl, every lap, was driving Naomi crazy, she just couldn't keep quiet. Her hands gripped onto Marquise's head full of waves, encouraging him to get deep inside. She couldn't help but push him deeper. She wanted more. He was providing her with so much pleasure and he hardly knew her. But still it seemed like he knew her body so well.

Naomi bit into her soft lips, as Marquise lapped at her pussy in fast, gentle licks, slow twirls and didn't hesitate once her juices started flowing.

"Tell me how much you like this shit Nicole," he ordered firmly, pushing his two fingers deeper and deeper inside her. Even though the moment was great for Naomi right now, things felt slightly awkward for her when she realized that she had given him a fake name. But there was no way that she was spoiling the moment by giving him her real name right now. That would have to wait for now.

"Answer me baby!" he demanded loudly, speeding up his finger motions. Faster and faster.

"It feels good! Uhhh, really good Marquise..."

"That's good baby. Tonight I wan' hear you tell me exactly how I'm makin' yo' pretty ass feel. Don't be shy... Especially when I'm dickin' you down," he said, before his wet tongue lapped and sucked back on her pussy.

***

"Take all yo' clothes off," he ordered firmly. "Now."

Naomi looked up as she sat on the edge of his red king-sized bed and began obeying his orders. She hadn't even had a chance to admire his bedroom décor properly because of the dim lights, and with Marquise's quick way of starting their sexual night. She quickly slipped off her heels and dress, leaving her in nothing but her lace bra. Her panties had disappeared after Marquise had made her orgasm, not once, not twice, but three times – against his apartment wall.

Watching her strip naked had Marquise's desire for this woman only growing stronger and stronger. Admiring her sexy naked body, he licked and bit his lips sexily, staring down her covered breasts, flat stomach, freshly shaven pussy, thick thighs and long legs. *Fuck, she's perfect!* Once she was naked, he didn't hesitate getting naked for her.

Naomi swore she almost fainted once he revealed those muscles to her. His attractive milk chocolate body had her eyes bulging out her sockets. She couldn't stop staring at those muscular arms, endless abs, perfect pecs and that big… long… thick… "Damn."

Marquise chuckled lightly at the way she had been eyeing his body and now that he had pulled off his pants and boxers, her eyes were on his dick. And hearing that quiet "Damn" only made him more excited for how he was about to show her how damn good his dick was.

Before reaching for a condom, Marquise decided that the best thing would be to remind this pretty woman of what was going down tonight.

"Look, Nicole," he began with a small sigh, gently tearing his magnum packet between his teeth, "this ain't just a quickie thing tonight baby girl. I'm fuckin' you all night, my way, every position, every minute until you can't stand no more. A'ight?"

All Naomi found herself doing was nodding shyly at him before sighing softly. There was no way that she was backing out now. Not now that she was craving him, badly, and not a single doubt in her mind was lingering around anymore. She had to do this for her.

Five minutes later, Naomi's lace bra had been removed off her body with a single touch by Marquise, and her legs were now hiked up around his torso while he gently kissed her soft lips.

Once she felt the hard tip of his shaft slowly push past her wet pussy lips, her lips broke away from his. Holding his seductive, hazel eyes, Naomi passionately moaned. A moan mixed with both pleasure and pain.

"Relax baby," he said, giving her hips a light squeeze, as he leaned his hips forward, slowly penetrating her soft core. He knew that she was probably experiencing slight pain because of his big size, so he kept it gentle on her… for now.

He exhaled against her warm mouth, easing his dick inside of her as much as she would allow on the first go. He lifted his right hand to gently stroke her thigh, feeling her tight resistance.

"Baby, relax… *Shit…*" He pulled back his hips, slowly working himself inside of her little by little. "Am I hurtin' you, ma?"

Naomi swore she saw stars. She swore she did because there's no way that this feeling was real. She had to be seeing stars, confirming to her that this was a dream. The pain mixed with pleasure was insanely amazing. "Uhh… It's okay, you're not," she whispered against his lips, reassuring him that the pain she felt was brief. She didn't want him to think he was hurting her which would probably make him stop. And she certainly didn't want to stop.

Naomi began spreading her legs further apart for him. She leaned into his hand that stroked her thigh and eased her body against the bed, breathing slowly as her muscles relaxed. "Mmm…"

His dick pulled back from her slippery pussy, slowly inching back inside her. The more he let himself settle inside her, the less the pain occurred and the more the pleasure seeped through.

"Marquise... Shit..." Her hips started rocking with his, wanting to feel more of him deep inside her.

"Yo' pussy so tight and shit," he softly exhaled, kissing along her soft cheek and down to her neck. She was so damn tight, pleasuring Marquise all the way.

"It feels... so... fucking good," she responded with a louder moan, surprising herself further with her cursing. She wasn't one to curse during sex. She continued to moan, pushing her round breasts against his chest as he placed his arm under her back. His slow thrusts helped her adjust better to his big dick.

Her tight walls relaxed around his condom covered dick, hugging it perfectly inside her. She dug her nails into his muscular back as he pushed even deeper past her tight pussy.

"Ugh! Marquise," she moaned against his ear, moving her lips to his temple, turning her head to meet his lips. She instantly pulled his hips closer to her, moving her body with his. Her legs rocked back and forth along his sides, panting quicker, as she took more of his hard, long length inside her.

She slipped her tongue past his lips, massaging their wet flesh together. The hot sucking noises of his dick, pulling out of her warm pussy sounded insanely sexy to Naomi.

Marquise groaned as her fingernails pressed firmly into his back. He suddenly pulled away from her lips and grabbed her chin only to demand, "Say my name."

And when she immediately obeyed, his body flooded with heat when she whispered hotly into his ear, "You're making me feel so good right now... Fuck me faster Marquise..."

When Naomi moved her hips quicker in rhythm with his, Marquise thrust his thick length inside of her quicker. He slid his hands up and down along her thighs, hugging her legs close to his sides, increasing the pleasurable friction of their every movement together. He parted his lips against hers, snaking and twisting his tongue around hers as they passionately kissed.

"Agh...Damnn," he groaned in-between their kiss, his muscles tightening as he eased in and out of her, faster.

Naomi couldn't control the loud moans leaving her lips. Their sex just felt too good. Way better than the sex she usually had. The bed creaked loudly underneath them, the headboard roughly rocking against the wall as Marquise increased the speed of his smooth thrusts.

"Agh...God, don't stop," she whimpered, still moving her hands to clutch and claw on to his muscular back. Her legs hiked up even higher over his hips when he grabbed her thighs, pulling them tighter to his sides.

"Uhh... Squeeze it... Squeeze it with yo' pussy just like that baby."

She closed her eyes, licking her soft lips as the overwhelming pleasure surged through her, throbbing deeply between her legs and she did as Marquise wished, clenching her walls tightly.

She buried her face against his neck, sucking and kissing at his heated skin. They both felt hot to the touch, burning up with lust and passion for each other. The quicker he pumped his thick shaft inside her, the closer she felt to her own release.

She clenched her tight walls, trying to hold off as long as she could, wanting to treasure every second of Marquise thrusting into her.

"I-I'm getting closer," she moaned, rocking her hips faster and harder.

Marquise was pleased to hear how vocal this woman was; to hear how much pleasure he was giving to her. He adjusted his hands to rest on her hips, pumping himself between her legs faster and harder, according to her eager cries.

He shuddered as her lips touched his neck, teasing one of his most sensitive spots. What the hell was she doing to him?

"That's right... Fuckin' cum for me baby," he groaned, pulling her hips tightly against his, the temperature climbing underneath his skin as their bodies moved together on top of the bed sheets. "Cum on my dick."

He could feel her walls tightening more and more around him, signaling that she was getting close to her fourth climax of the night. The fourth of many more to come.

"Marquise... I'm gonna cum..." He nodded quickly at her, listening to her sexy moans. He pecked her lips and slowly trailed kisses down toward her collarbone.

"And that's all you gon' be doin' all night baby… cummin' for me," he whispered passionately in her left ear.

***

Marquise used one hand to grab hold of her curvy hips and another to slap her round ass, rubbing his wet tip faster between her pussy lips.

"Shit," she whimpered. He had her on her knees, hands pressed on the bed in front of her with him watching that sexy, fat ass of hers. Naomi had never had to go on all fours when it came to sex, but doing it now was turning her on. He slowly pushed his thick length inside her, completely filling her up with his big dick.

"Oooo...Marquise, shit." Her moans just couldn't be concealed, and once he started moving, neither could his. In and out he pounded inside her, watching her take it all. Her ass jiggled as he eased in and out of her, his deep thrusts and strokes getting faster by the minute.

"Yes baby...fuck me!" She felt so good around his shaft– tight, firm, and getting wetter by the second. "Harder Marquise...fuck yes..." He had brought out a side of her she never knew she could show before.

"God damn...this how you want it, baby?" he groaned deeply, pulling his dick back out and quickly pushing it back in again. "This how you wan' all this dick?" Her legs shook as he pushed into her, slamming their bodies together and watching that fat ass of hers that he loved so much, jiggle back and forth.

The hard smacking noise of their bodies colliding together, moans, and groans echoed in the bedroom. "Twerk your fat ass on this dick ma'...yeah...just like that."

He tightened his hold on her hips, watching as her ass moved. He kept rocking her body hard, back and forward on his dick. He groaned deep with each thrust, roughly massaging his hands against her hot skin. With each fast pump of his hips, Marquise felt like he was going to lose control and burst.

"You tryna break my dick girl…"

***

He fell back onto the bed without hesitation and licked his lips, watching her drop between his legs. He sexily bit his lip when her manicured nails raked along his thighs, inching closer to his thick dick.

Naomi really couldn't believe she was about to do this right now. She hardly sucked dick but something about the way that Marquise had stretched and bent her in various positions already made her want to take things to the next level.

He shuddered lightly when her warm tongue licked the swollen tip of his dick. He sucked in a quick breath the moment her warm mouth started to devour his long length. "Fuck, Nicole…" Marquise instantly grabbed a fistful of her brown hair, guiding her head up and down, groaning louder the further her perfect mouth took him inside her warm, tight mouth.

His head fell back against the bed, closing his eyes and enjoying the heavenly feel of her hot mouth, sucking him hard. The more she sucked, the more she filled her mouth with his massive length without a hint of hesitation. His dick was so big it was like a foot was in her mouth. And Naomi loved every single bit of it.

Both his hands reached into her soft hair, curling it around his fists. He grunted deep, lifting her head up and down, rhythmically pulling her up and down at his speed. "Take all this dick… Just like that girl," he groaned, gently pumping his thick length into her mouth.

His eyes opened, looking down at her as she continued to take his dick deeper and deeper into her mouth. Their eyes locked and it made his dick twitch hard against her tongue. Her mouth felt amazing on him, he just loved everything about the way she was sucking him off. Warm, smooth and tight. She was so nasty. So freaky.

She had a look of excitement in her eyes. She was enjoying herself. "Uhh... Nicole... You bad girl." He squeezed her hair in his hand, groaning roughly and dropping his head back against the bed.

His eyes rolled up to the back of his head as her mouth worked his wet dick. He gently pumped his hips up and down, now pushing his length deep down her throat. She took it all. She was the best woman who had ever given him head, he knew that for sure. She was skilled and attentive to his dick and knew how to please him effortlessly. "Feels so good baby..."

Marquise looked down at her, exhaling when her mouth popped off his hard dick. Her hand pumped his thick length as she gazed up at him with a hint of his pre-cum on her glossy lips.

"Baby, come ride me backwards." He didn't want to cum just yet as that would make their sweet moment together quickly finish. He wanted their fucking session to last as long as they could make it last.

She slowly got up, reached for the condom nearby on the bed, placed it on his bare muscular chest before she licked her lips seductively at him. She climbed on top of him, turning around so that her back was now towards him.

Once he had wrapped up, Naomi gently guided his thick dick to her entrance, teasing her wet folds with the head of his dick. The feel of his wet tip against her sensitive clit felt like ecstasy. Heaven on earth in fact.

He smoothed his hand over her firm ass, rubbing his palm up and down her warm skin. He couldn't help but bite on his bottom lip when she pushed her ass out further, looking over at him seductively. "Nicole... I swear you the baddest freak I ever been wit," he teased her, delivering a playful slap to her ass cheeks, ready to be inside her so badly.

"I'm your freaky girl Marquise," she stated confidently, only making Marquise light up with happiness. He then slapped her ass a little harder, watching her rub his tip faster between her soaked lips. The shit looked sexy as fuck. He needed to be inside her but he wanted her to have control.

She slowly pushed his long length inside her, filling herself up until his whole dick disappeared into her tight slit.

"Baby... Uhhh... Fuck," he groaned deep, as she pulled his dick back out her pussy and slowly pushed it back in again. "Damn baby... Yes...Ride this fuckin' dick... It's yours."

"Uhh God... All mine?"

"All yours, freaky girl."

CHAPTER 5 ~ REGRETFUL DECISIONS

4.45am.

They had just finished fucking forty-five minutes ago and Marquise had passed out with Naomi in his arms and tears now falling down her cheeks.

What the fuck have I done? She had slept with another man that wasn't her man. A man that wasn't her husband, wasn't the love of her life and definitely wasn't the father of her kids. She had let another man touch her in places he wasn't supposed to fucking touch, and let him kiss her like she belonged to him. She had freely fucked him, in all types of ways, positions and stances. Positions she dared not try with Tyree because he liked missionary, and missionary alone.

I need to get home! Tyree's going to be worried. Even though I told him to not wait up for me... Now Naomi had regretted going out in the first place. She had definitely felt like a hoe, fucking a man that she had just met. She had used condoms with him but so what? She still needed to go get checked up and make sure that she was free of anything before she slept with Tyree again.

Naomi slowly shuffled her naked body out of Marquise's arms, trying her hardest not to wake him up. She didn't want to wake him up and then have him asking her questions and only fucking her brains out again to get her to stay. He couldn't even anyway. The only reason why they had stopped fucking was because they had run out of condoms and Naomi was feeling sore. So before deciding to pass out, Marquise poured some wine, smoked a blunt, let Naomi have a smoke, and kissed her lovingly before hitting the sack.

The moment she was up out of his bed and free, she instantly searched for her clothes and put them on. She knew that the minute she got home she would have to take a shower and brush her teeth. A shower would wash his kisses, his touch and brushing would remove the taste of his dick from her mouth. The taste that she had loved sucking, licking and swallowing…

Naomi took one last look at the handsome man sleeping naked so peacefully on his bed. "Goodbye sexy stranger… Thanks for a great night," she whispered sadly, before quietly turning on her heels out his room.

***

"Baby, I'm sorry about being so hard on you about going out… I understand you're a grown woman and should be allowed to let your hair down sometimes," Tyree explained, moving closer to Naomi on their shared bed.

Thank God she had managed to take a shower and brush before waking Tyree up. She hoped he would be fast asleep but hearing her enter their en-suite bathroom had woken him up.

"It's okay… I didn't need to go out anyway," she responded quietly, feeling a big wave of guilt quiver through her because of what she had done with Marquise the whole night. A small wave of lust also quivered through her due to the explicit images she could picture of him fucking her, eating her out, fingering her, sucking her nipp-

"No sweetheart," Tyree stated warmly, grabbing hold of her hand. "I'm your husband, and I understand that you have needs when it comes to hanging with your girls. You can't always be cooped up here at home with the kids and I. You work so hard at work every day and I should never stop you from trying to relax. I want you to be happy. See how I ain't even trip about you coming home now? I love you and want you to be happy. If that means going out with your girls when you feel like it, then so be it. I shouldn't stop you from being happy."

"Tyree, honestly it's not a big de-" Her words were instantly cut off when Tyree branded his lips to hers. Even kissing him felt guilty and weird. She'd rather it be Marquise kissing her, and rubbing on her booty while he did it, too.

Snap out of it girl! She couldn't be thinking about a complete stranger while kissing her husband, her children's father, the love her life. It wasn't right and fair to him.

Yet, as he continued to kiss her, she couldn't find it in her heart to whole heartedly return the kiss. All the while she continued to think about Marquise's soft lips upon hers and his hands roaming all over her body.

Tyree hovered above her while staring into her eyes lovingly. His heart ached at the thought of upsetting his wife and the only thing he wanted at this moment was her forgiveness. Naomi had never relented against her advances and although she didn't say no, he could tell that she just wasn't into it.

Oh my God, he knows! He knows that I've been with someone else. Naomi thought as she avoided his gaze. Her heart was beating a mile a minute while Tyree continued to stare at her. Moments seemed like a lifetime as complete panic set in.

"Tyree, I-" Naomi began before she was cut off by Tyree.

"Baby, please don't be mad at me. I know it's late and you're probably tired, but I just want to hold you," Tyree admitted while wrapping his arms around Naomi and drawing her near.

Even his embrace felt foreign as she relented and allowed him to hold her. She buried her face in his chest and tears stung her eyes. She couldn't let him see how this was affecting her because she wasn't sure if she would be able to look him in the eyes and lie to him.

"I love you baby," Tyree said as he gently kissed her forehead.

"I love you, too," Naomi replied softly as she allowed the now tainted words to leave her lips. How could she ever say them again after what she had done? Did she really love her husband as much as she thought, after completely giving herself to a stranger?

Naomi closed her eyes and allowed herself to drift off to sleep, all the while thinking of Marquise and allowing herself to put the night behind her. After all she would never see him again and she was never going back to that club.

***

The next morning, Naomi was up and out of bed before Tyree. She managed to take a bath and cook breakfast for the kids without waking him. She had gotten them dressed and dropped them off at his mother's house as promised the night before. She was so zoned out while placing his plate of food on the table, that she hadn't heard him enter the room. She was pouring his orange juice when he walked up behind her and wrapped his arms around her waist. She jumped, almost dropping the glass vase she used to store the juice.

"I'm sorry baby, I didn't mean to scare you," Tyree admitted as he kissed the side of her neck.

"No, it's fine babe. It's not your fault," Naomi responded while placing the vase on the table.

"You did all this for me baby?" Tyree asked as he peeped around her at the table.

"Yes sweetie. I promised we would spend some time together and I wanted to make sure I followed through," she explained.

Tyree smiled while making his way to his plate and Naomi took a seat directly across from him. He dug in, immediately inhaling all of the food she made. She took a sip of orange juice from her glass and stared at her plate. She popped a piece of strawberry into her mouth while forcing herself to swallow it. She felt sick to her stomach right now, and the car ride home from dropping off the kids didn't help like she thought it would.

"Babe, you okay over there?" Tyree managed to ask in-between bites.

"Uh yeah. I think I drank a little too much last night. Do you mind if I lay down for a little while?" Naomi questioned.

"You never could handle your liquor," he chuckled while chugging orange juice.

Naomi grinned, pushing her chair back and attempting to stand. She grabbed her plate, making her way to the microwave to place it inside for later.

"Hey, I have to run out for a minute to help Evan at the little league game. But, I'll be back as soon as it's over," Tyree said.

"Okay that's fine, and take all the time you need," she replied while making her way up the stairs. She stepped inside of her bedroom slightly closing the door behind her and walked to her bathroom. She turned on the water and splashed it onto her face while taking a deep breath. She then stared at her reflection momentarily before stepping back into her bedroom.

She pulled the covers back and slid underneath before throwing them over her head. She sighed while closing her eyes. *Okay girl, get it together. You did a bad thing that felt so good, but it's over. You have a husband who loves you and a beautiful family. If he found out it would ruin your marriage. It was a one-night stand and nothing more, so forget about it and move on,* Naomi told herself. She allowed herself to drift off into a peaceful slumber and free itself of guilt for the time being.

CHAPTER 6 ~ FORBIDDEN FRUIT

Naomi managed to make it through the entire day without allowing the guilt of her deception to overwhelm her. She catered to Tyree and spent some much needed quality time with her husband. Although he had tried to become intimate with her, she simply had to decline by telling him that she wasn't feeling well. It was one thing to cheat on her husband, but she wasn't going to sleep with him until she was evaluated by a physician. She made an appointment and by the grace of God, they had a consultation the next day.

She would have to leave work early, but she had no other choice. Besides, she made sure to always be there for her students and hardly ever called off of work. Once she did, all would be right in the world. She contemplated admitting her wrong doings to her husband once some time had passed, but quickly decided against it. She simply wasn't willing to lose her family for a mistake that would never happen again. Besides, men did shit like this all the time right?

Naomi was currently standing in line waiting to order her latte at a small local coffee shop. Once upon a time, she had come here pretty often to unwind or when she just needed a moment to herself. It was a safe place for her and she enjoyed the view of people walking about and enjoying their everyday life. She smiled as she stepped up to the counter to place her order, paid for her drink, and patiently waited for her order to be completed.

Naomi grabbed her coffee and headed to the seat closest to the window. She inhaled the aroma while allowing it to fill her senses. She glanced out of the window while sipping her coffee and smiled at the people passing by. A little girl clutched her mother's hand as they walked down the street to a local restaurant. She continued to watch while two elderly women passed by the window in a full-blown conversation, smiling from ear to ear.

She smiled as they passed the window and began searching for the next passer-by. As she looked out the window, she noticed the two elderly women crossing the street further down and noticed a dark truck sitting outside where two men stood. She continued to watch and almost looked in a different direction until one of the men turned around.

Naomi felt her heart skip a beat as she laid eyes on Marquise. She sunk further in her seat, praying that he wouldn't head in her direction and happen to see her sitting there. She blew out a breath while Marquise climbed inside of his truck and began to drive in her direction. She quickly grabbed a magazine that sat on her table and buried her face inside of it. Her heart was beating so fast that she was sure it would jump out of her chest.

She sat there completely still until she was sure that he was nowhere in sight. Naomi then stood, grabbing her coffee and making a quick exit to her car. Once she was inside, she let out the breath that she had been holding since the moment she laid eyes on him. She closed her eyes as the images of the night she spent with him came flooding back to her memory.

God that man had done some things to her body that she had never imagined possible. She had been trying so desperately to forget, but it was nearly impossible because she just couldn't forget. She knew that it would take some time, but the only way that she would be able to forget was if she didn't have to see him again. She knew that the odds were in her favor considering she hardly went anywhere, but she knew that there was always a small chance.

Naomi started her car and pulled into traffic completely consumed in her thoughts. How could she allow herself to be so frazzled? She had to get it together not only for her sake, but for her family. If she continued to act so paranoid, surely Tyree would notice and began to become suspicious. She had to block every memory, moment, and amazing feeling Marquise had given her from her mind. She had to stay away from that man at all costs.

***

Naomi was observing her class once again during recess while Erin chattered away about the man she met during their girl's night out. With every word that Erin spoke, Naomi slipped deeper and deeper into her thoughts of Marquise. She thought about confiding in Erin about Marquise, but quickly decided against it. Although her best friend loved her and would support her no matter what, she didn't want to see the look of disappointment in her eyes that she was almost certain would be there.

"Hello? Earth to Naomi. Have you heard anything I said girl?" Erin asked as she stood in her line of vision.

"Oh sorry. What did you say?" Naomi asked.

"Girl, what is up with you today? You have been totally zoned out. Are you okay?" Erin questioned.

"I'm fine Erin, just a little tired. I haven't been feeling all that well and it's causing me to be a little distracted, that's all," Naomi admitted.

"You sure?" Erin eyed her skeptically.

"Yea', I'll be fine. Now finish telling me about your little boy toy," Naomi encouraged.

Erin laughed while describing the night's details. Naomi did well with pretending to listen and being completely enthralled in their conversations. All the while, Naomi swam in images of the night she spent with her own man candy, Marquise.

After being thoroughly examined by her doctor and receiving an all clear, Naomi had managed to have sex with her husband. She relented after multiple attempts after still not feeling okay with being intimate with him. She soon realized that sex with him would never be the same after the insane amount of pleasure Marquise was able to give her.

Even the slightest touch from Tyree did absolutely nothing for her. She found herself imagining that Tyree was Marquise in order to get wet and be intimate with him at all. She had to relive that night over and over in her mind because no matter what she could never do it again. Marquise had become her forbidden fruit and she just could not indulge.

She never knew that someone could change her whole outlook and perspective on life within just one night. Marquise had completely turned her world upside down and she had done nothing to stop it. Absolutely nothing.

***

Even at a tense time like this, Marquise couldn't concentrate as well as he usually could. He just couldn't. All because of *her*.

"It wasn't us, Blaze! Please! We're being set u-"

"Shut yo' ass up," Blaze spat, giving him another few hard whips with his black Versace belt. "Tired of you fuckin' beggin'... when you know... you and yo' crew... fucked up!" Blaze exclaimed crazily in between his whips before deciding that it was time to end this fool. Marquise couldn't stand this stupid idiot begging and shit. This is the type of bullshit that pissed him off. Niggas begging when they knew that they had brought themselves in their own shit.

"Blaze, please... Don't kill me ma-"

"We know it was yo' crew that robbed us," Kareem announced boldly, interrupting Donte's pleads. "Stop lyin' man... You just making this shit worse."

"Shoulda never let yo' homies attack us," Marquise snapped, angrily kicking Donte in the stomach, resulting in him to crouch forward in pain and cough up some more blood. Marquise was fuming mostly about the fact that his crew, Knight Nation had been attacked in the first place. He couldn't believe that The Lyons, their archenemies had had the audacity to actually come for their empire.

Due to the whippings from Blaze's belt, punches from Kareem and kicks from Marquise, Donte was covered in bruises, scars and cuts everywhere. He was shirtless too, so the belt, punches and kicks were hitting his chest, face, stomach and back.

Donte was a member of the Lyons, Leek's crew. The same crew that Blaze's Knight Nation just didn't fuck with. Matter of fact, they hated each other. So it made sense for them to try and attack and stupidly leave their signature gang tag 'LYONS RULE' at the scene of the attacked trap house.

"We endin' this shit now. No more tryin' to come for us. You stupid little niggas way out yo' league anyways, tryna come for us all the damn time," Blaze stated with a smirk, as he lifted the butt of his gun to the side of Donte's bloody head. "Say night night, nigga."

This nigga and his corny shit... Marquise began to chuckle and Blaze turned his head to stare at him. "Why you laughin' nigga?"

"You always got some corny shit to say B'," he responded with another chuckle. That's one of the things he loved about his boy. Always trying to poke fun of a sticky situation whenever he could.

Blaze laughed lightly before turning to Kareem, still pressing the butt of his gun hard into the side of Donte's head.

"Yo Reem, you think I always got some corny shit to say?"

"Sometimes nigga... But I guess that's jus' you," he said with a shrug.

"Hmm, I hear you," Blaze stated before turning around to a petrified Donte. "Donte, you think I always got some corny shit to say?"

Donte kept silent and just looked up with tears forming in his brown eyes.

"He asked you a fuckin' question boy," Marquise barked, about to deliver a kick to Donte, when Blaze stopped him with a firm hand to his chest.

"Chill Marq... He'll answer it in his own time," Blaze announced calmly. "What'chu got to say Donte? Think I say some corny shit?

Donte took a deep breath and blinked a few times before deciding to break his scared silence. "I don't... know."

"Take a wild guess nigga," Blaze cajoled him sternly.

Donte sighed deeply before responding, "No, you ain't got corn-"

Pow! Pow! Pow!

Donte never got a chance to finish because Blaze had blown his brains out, resulting in Donte's dead body to fall back and spurt out a never ending flow of his blood. "Wrong answer motherfucker," Blaze concluded confidently with a sinister smile. "I always got corny shit to say once in a while."

Even at a time like this, Marquise still couldn't fucking concentrate! Ever since he had had her, that night… all he could think about was having her again and again and again. It was her fault that he couldn't stop thinking about her. He wanted to feel those hands touching on his body again, rubbing on that sexy body of hers, and feel that tight pussy of hers riding his dick all night.

But he couldn't. Nicole had left him with nothing. Not a number, not an address, not an e-mail, not an Instagram, not a Twitter. Absolutely nothing. And the shit had left him pissed off once he realized that there was no way of getting in contact with her.

She had turned into a forbidden fruit. Something that he wanted but couldn't have. Nicole was now an absolute stranger to him and her whereabouts completely unknown.

CHAPTER 7 ~ CRAVING YOU

Naomi sat in the cozy Italian restaurant that both her and Erin had been dying to try. For months they'd been talking about coming to the restaurant and when Erin suggested the restaurant for the girl's day as opposed to the club they recently visited, she almost jumped for joy. She knew that telling Erin what took place was completely out of the question, even though she contemplated it a million times. It wasn't that she didn't trust her best friend, Naomi just wanted to forget that the night ever happened and that meant keeping it to herself so that no one could remind her.

Things between her and Tyree had almost gotten back to normal. She was now able to deal with that fact that she'd cheated on her husband. What helped her sleep at night was the fact that it was a one-time thing. She promised herself that she would never do something so crazy ever again. Despite it all, she still found herself having dreams about Marquise. Naomi would have sporadic flashbacks of their night together.

Naomi's thoughts were interrupted as Erin approached the table.

"Hey girl! Sorry I'm late," Erin offered as she set her purse down and slid in the booth.

"Girl, you are never on time. I know you didn't think I thought you were going to change that today," Naomi chuckled.

Erin gave her the finger while Naomi pretended to be shocked. "Well beauty takes time hunny," Erin laughed.

"So what's been up with you? Any new love interests?" Naomi asked while the waitress brought fresh water and bread with an Italian herb butter.

"Well, the little cutie I met at the club has been tearing my line down, girl, practically begging for another night with me. Of course he'll never get it, though," Erin laughed.

"Well why not Erin? You're both single and like you said before, it was good, so what's the problem?" Naomi replied.

"For one he's far too young for my taste and why do we have to make it personal? I want things to remain strictly physical, and of course here he comes blurting out that he wants more," Erin replied before the waitress came to take their order.

Naomi laughed while shaking her head at her best friend. Clearly she had some issues when it came to the love department. However, Naomi knew what she'd been through so she understood why Erin chose to take that approach when it came to the opposite sex.

"My god you are such a dude Erin," Naomi laughed as the waitress left the table to prepare their food.

"I know and I'm perfectly fine with that. Men do it all the time so why should I waste my time believing their bullshit when we both know that they're lying just to get into my pants. Why not just be two adults who know what they want, that way there won't be any misconceptions or misunderstandings?" Erin offered.

"I hear you, but you're still young. You don't want to have kids and a family? Get married and find the one man that you'll spend the rest of your life with?" Naomi questioned.

"Uh, no, and you already know that. I like being exactly who I am and I honestly don't believe that there is any man out there that will change that. I mean I love kids, I'm a teacher for God's sake. But, there are too many heartaches and disappointments when it comes to dating and I just don't want to be bothered," Erin explained.

Naomi nodded her head in agreement. She knew exactly what Erin was getting at and she knew the struggle all too well. Being a wife and mother was hard work and it was simply your life's work.

"I hear ya, girl. Well you can always come and get my little monsters whenever you'd like," Naomi chuckled.

"Oh yea', my babies love them some tete Erin! You know I'm their favorite," Erin laughed as she did a happy dance in her seat.

"Yes we-" Naomi said as her words were cut off.

"Hey, isn't that Marquise, the guy from the club?" Erin asked as she slightly leaned and glanced behind Naomi at a group of men walking towards them.

"Oh shit," Naomi said as she scooted down in her side of the seat. This could not be happening after all she'd promised herself. *Fuck, not again. This cannot be happening!*

"Girl, what in the hell is wrong with you?" Erin asked as she eyed Naomi suspiciously.

"Nothing, I just don't want him to see me, that's all," Naomi admitted.

"And why not? Did that nigga do something to you? Because you know I don't have a problem with fucking his ass up," Erin said as she leaned forward to carefully inspect her friend.

"No, it wasn't anything like that Erin, I promise," Naomi stated.

"Are you sure? Because I don't care how big him and his friends are. I'll still kick his ass," Erin clarified.

"It's okay really. Now can you please stop looking that way before he notices you?" Naomi said.

"Nope, not until you tell me why you really don't want to see him," Erin declared.

Naomi bit down on her bottom lip while contemplating if she should tell her friend the real truth about what happened between her and Marquise. She really didn't want to get anyone involved in the mess that she'd created of her own life, and the only way to do that was to lie.

"Okay fine. I made a fool out of myself that night. I was drunk and flirting with him when I had no business whatsoever doing that. I spilled a drink on him, too, by accident when he tried to kiss me," Naomi lied while fainting embarrassment.

"Oh my God! Really Naomi? For the record, flirting is not cheating girl. It's only when you act on it that it becomes cheating and we both know you love Tyree," Erin declared.

"Yeah, you're right," Naomi said reluctantly, as their food was brought to the table and placed in front of them. She was at a loss for words as Erin ate and continued to chat. Every now and then, she'd chime in a few words so that she'd know that she was paying attention, but refused to readdress the Marquise situation. How would her friend feel if she'd known that she had cheated on her husband? Yes, she did love Tyree, but sex with Marquise had been the most amazing thing she'd ever encountered in her life. Here he was, once again in the same place as her. What are the odds that she'd keep running into him after never laying eyes on him before? She didn't know why, but what she did know was that she had to make it out of that restaurant without him seeing her.

***

"Are they still there?" Naomi asked.

"No girl, I told you they ate like a bunch of hungry hippos and left about five minutes ago.

"Are you sure?" Naomi responded.

"Yes, I'm sure. Why don't you turn around and see for yourself if you don't believe me?" Erin replied.

Slowly, Naomi turned towards the table behind her that Marquise and his friends had been sitting at. The table was completely empty and was filled with empty food plates.

"Thank God," Naomi said as she turned around to face her friend.

"Girl, Atlanta is only so big. You bound to run into that man again and when you do, don't run. Try speaking and say hello—you'd be surprised what he might say. Besides, you can have friends, girl, just let him know that you guys will be friends and nothing more," Erin said.

"I need to use the restroom before we leave," Naomi said as she slid out of the booth and stood up. She grabbed her purse and began searching for her wallet.

"Girl, put that thing away. It's my treat this time," Erin smiled warmly.

"Thanks girl. I'll be right back," Naomi smiled back, as she made her way to the bathroom. Naomi pushed the door open and stepped inside. She went to the first empty stall she found and relieved her bladder.

She stepped out of the stall, walked to the sink, and began washing her hands. She stared at her reflection in the mirror and closed her eyes. Images of Marquise and his mouth on her pussy flooded her brain, causing her to instantly become wet. She exhaled as she tried to regain her composure and talk some sense into herself. *Never again Naomi. We cannot go there again.*
Finally, she dried her hands and exited the bathroom making her way back to their table. Erin was grabbing her purse as she approached the table.
"Let's go girl," Erin said while walking to the door. Naomi was right behind her as they stepped out into the night. She told herself that she was going to leave the thoughts of Marquise and that night in the past where they belonged.

CHAPTER 8 ~ NOT LETTING YOU GO

"Call you later okay? I got a date," Erin said.

"A date, huh? Who's the not so lucky guy tonight?" Naomi chuckled.

"I beg your pardon? Any nigga who get with me is lucky, okay?" Erin laughed. It was only when Naomi suddenly reached into her bag that she realized she was missing something.

"Shit, I forgot my cell phone inside the bathroom! I have to go back," Naomi said as she frantically dug deeper in her purse to make sure it wasn't there.

"Okay, I'll wait for you," Erin said.

"No, you go ahead. I'll be fine," Naomi demanded.

"Are you sure girl? You know I will," Erin questioned.

"Really, it's fine girl. Go ahead. I'll call you when I make it home," Naomi called over her shoulder as she entered back into the restaurant.

Naomi maneuvered her way to the restaurant and entered the bathroom to find it sitting in the exact same place she'd left it.

Thank God! I don't know what I would have done without my damn phone! Naomi thought as she exited the bathroom and made her way to door. She stepped back outside and walked towards her car. But as she approached it, she could see a figure leaning up against the driver's side door.

She stopped dead in her tracks and squinted in an attempt to make out the face. She wasn't stupid by a long shot, so there was no way she was going to walk up on someone that big at this time of night.

"You got five seconds to get the fuck off of my car or else I'm calling the police," Naomi yelled.

The man stood and began walking towards her. "What, you don't miss me?" he said.

She knew that voice all too well. It was same voice that made her pussy dripping wet at just the very first thought of him. It was the same voice of the man who had managed to creep into her dreams every night since the moment they'd met. Marquise was right in front of her and this time there was nowhere for her to hide. *Shit.*

"What are you doing?" Naomi asked as she began to walk back towards her car.

"Did you think I wouldn't recognize your friend, ma'?" Marquise asked, following quickly behind her.

"I don't know," Naomi asked as she came to a complete stop in front of him.

"Nicole, why did you leave without tellin' me? How am I supposed to get in contact with you?" Marquise asked.

Naomi's pussy throbbed just from looking at him. Marquise looked even better than before as he stood in front of her. Clad in dark blue jeans, a red checkered shirt, Timberlands, two silver chains and a diamond stud in each ear. Marquise was looking fine, real fine! This man was truly God's gift to women. She still felt weird at the fact that he was calling her by the fake name that she had given him the first night they had met. But oh well. She was just going to have to get used to it.

"You weren't supposed to. Isn't that the whole point of a one-night stand?" Naomi questioned as she stepped around him and moved to open the door.

"That depends on if that's all you want it to be shorty," Marquise declared, stopping her from completely opening her door and shutting it close.

"No strings attached," Naomi said as she forced her face to remain relaxed. If only he knew what he was doing to her every time he stepped closer and closer.

"Really? Because I don't believe you Nicole," Marquise said as he stepped closer and repositioned his body to where it was standing as close as humanly possible. Naomi found herself pushed up against her car door with Marquise standing right in front of her.

Naomi's breath hitched as Marquise put one hand on the car beside her face. "What, you thought I was done fuckin' wit'chu?" he questioned firmly. "Nah baby... I'm just gettin' fuckin' started with yo' sexy ass. Ain't no way I'm lettin' that bomb ass pussy of yours go." He then brought his face as close as possible while his other hand made its way to her stomach. Marquise gently kissed her, sending electricity through her body. His hand made its way to the top of her pants while Naomi returned his kiss, allowing his tongue to enter her mouth.

Oh God this is bad... really, really bad, Naomi thought to herself. Even though she knew it was wrong, she couldn't form the words to tell him to stop. Everything about his hands being on her body felt so right. Naomi leaned into his kiss and allowed her hands to disappear under his shirt and onto his rock hard abs.

"Tell me you don't want to feel this dick again," Marquise demanded as his hands dove inside her pants and quickly began pushing her panties to the side. He worked his fingers through to her soft folds and gently stroked her clitoris.

"Ah!" Naomi moaned into his mouth while he inserted his fingers inside of her pussy.

"That's right baby. This pussy's mine, remember? Look how wet you are for me ma'," Marquise said as he worked his fingers faster. Naomi continued to passionately suck and lick on his bottom lip.

"Stop fightin' this shit girl... You know you wan' me, and I want you," he stated. "I'm the only one who fucks that pussy right. You still want to forget about me? 'Bout how good I fucked you all night baby?" Marquise said as he began to finger her right there in the middle of the parking lot.

"No! Ah!" Naomi cried as she felt her orgasm approaching.

"That's right Nicole. Cum for daddy right now," Marquise demanded and just like that, she did. Naomi crashed hard as the orgasm ripped through her body sending her into another world. Marquise continued to kiss her as her body came down from the high he had just given her. Naomi opened her eyes to find Marquise smiling from ear to ear. He then took those same fingers he used to finger her and stuck them in his mouth, sexily sucking her juices off of them.

Instantly, Naomi became wet again from the sight before her. She wanted Marquise so bad that her entire body was shaking.

"Ain't nobody gonna do that pussy like me Nicole. I need to feel you again and I won't take no for an answer, you hear me?" Marquise declared as he firmly kissed her again and their tongues entangled together.

Naomi leaned into him, gripping the back of his head to pull him closer. When they both came up for air, Marquise reached into his pocket and grabbed his business card. He then placed it into her hand and said, "Call me when you're ready for me baby. Don't keep me waitin' too long."

Marquise gently eased her to the side and opened her car door. He waited for her to climb inside before gently kissing her lips and closing the door behind her. A dazed Naomi started her car and looked at the card in her hand. She stuck it into her bra and put her car in reverse to turn around before making her way out of the parking lot.

Naomi reveled in the afterglow of what had just taken place. No matter how hard she'd tried to forget him, he always remained in the back of her thoughts. Marquise was by far the sexiest most demanding man she'd ever encountered. The way he made her feel was undeniable and the most amazing feeling in the world. It was in that moment that she realized that she was going to see Marquise again and she was going to fuck him like never before. Marquise had become her escape from reality and she was going to enjoy him for what he was worth in every possible way.

***

"9pm. Four seasons. You got it bae?"

"I got it."

"Don't be late baby."

7.35pm.

Naomi had been waiting for this night all week. Now that it had finally arrived it she was nervous as hell. Her heart wouldn't stop beating fast and her legs and hands wouldn't stop shaking. Even Tyree had noticed her nervous mood but she quickly assured him that there was nothing wrong with her and it was "that time of the month." By saying that, she wouldn't have to have sex with him anytime soon and after having sex with Marquise tonight, she wouldn't want Tyree touching any part of her.

"So where you going out again sweetheart?" Tyree suddenly questioned her, watching as she tightly tied her brown trench coat. She had managed to hide her clothes from him as she didn't want him seeing what she had underneath. What was underneath was for Marquise's eyes only.

"Just grabbing a few drinks with the girls hun," she responded simply with a weak smile. "And we're probably going to be out all night, so don't wait up."

"Are you sure? I could come pick you u-"

She quickly cut him off, "No Ty. Seriously, I'm good. I'll just catch an Uber."

"Why aren't you driving?"

"Because I'll be drinking and I don't want anything to happen on my way back babe," she explained gently. "Don't worry about me."

"Are you sure?" he asked sheepishly, moving to stand behind her.

"Yes baby," she said turning around to face him and lifting her hands to his shoulders. "Positive." She gave him a quick peck before moving away from his lips. "Don't wait up for m-" She was suddenly cut off mid-sentence when Tyree's lips locked down to hers.

In the past, his sweet kisses and attempts to make her to stay with him always worked. They always managed to ensure that he got his own way. But not today.

"Ty... No," Naomi voiced with a firm hand on his chest, stopping him from trying to kiss her further. "I really gotta go."

"Just stay with me tonight... We can have our own drinks babe," he whispered sexily in her ear and wrapped his arms around her waist. "Then do a couple of things... Some really bad things."

Naomi couldn't help but chuckle at her husband's dull attempt to make her stay. There was no way she was staying with him, having the same old drinks and doing the same old missionary position, over and over again.

Tonight she was doing exactly what she wanted.

CHAPTER 9 ~
ONCE A CHEATER, ALWAYS A CHEATER

Naomi sighed deeply before taking one last glance at the Four Seasons' hotel entrance. The bright lights enticed her to step out her Uber and enter inside. But for some reason, an indescribable feeling had come over her again.

What the hell was she doing?

She was a married woman. A married woman. But here she was, getting ready to meet a man who wasn't even her husband. A man that she hardly even knew.

Mom would be so disappointed in you Naomi. And Dad? He wouldn't even want to see you.

Naomi had been raised to be a good, kind and respectable young lady. She was taught to aspire to marriage and dreamt of having a man sweep her off her feet. Mother always said, "You need a man. Marriage is important, baby. It's joy and love and something you need." She had to believe that in order to live a happy life she needed to be married. She couldn't have too many boyfriends and she certainly couldn't go around sleeping with them all. She could only date a few and always make sure that marriage was the top priority in her mind.

So when Tyree came around, marriage was the first thing on her mind when she got with him. She wanted to be a loyal and loving wife. But how the fuck was her dressed in a trench coat, covering her half naked body, and sitting in a car outside a hotel room to meet a man that wasn't her husband, being a loyal and loving wife?

The more she contemplated on this whole situation, the more doubts filled her head. And within fifteen minutes of doubts swirling her head, Naomi figured the best thing to do would be to go home. That was until her phone vibrated in her bag, indicating a notification.

"We're here ma'am," the driver said.

"I know, but I'm not ready to go in yet," Naomi replied.

"Well you know that's going to be extra," the driver informed her.

"Of course and I'll pay whatever extra money I have to," Naomi responded gently.

She reached into her purse only to see an incoming text from Marquise.

"Where you at?"

"I don't think I can make it," she texted back slowly.

Marquise: *"What? Why not?"*

Naomi: *"I'm busy?"*

Marquise: *"You weren't busy an hour ago."*

Marquise: *"You lying."*

Shit. Naomi didn't like the fact that he could read her like a book even without staring into her eyes and hear the sound of her voice. She needed to think fast and quick.

Naomi: *"I'm sorry Marq... I'm busy tonight."*

She expected another quick reply from him but all that came was a small ID telling her that he had seen her message and nothing more. It wasn't until her driver started the car engine when her phone began to ring.

She looked down at the caller ID only to see that it was Marquise calling her. She knew she shouldn't have picked up. She shouldn't have! Because the next couple of sentences he said changed everything.

"Hello?"

"I don't care if you busy tonight... I want you, completely naked, in my bed tonight," he ordered over the phone. "I ain't takin' no for an answer. Don't make me come find yo' ass."

"Marquise, I really ca-"

He suddenly cut her off, "Get yo' ass out that car and in this fuckin' hotel Nicole."

Her heart almost froze on the spot. "What... What d-"

"What you thought I ain't kno' yo' ass been sitting in the car for almost an hour now Nicole? I own half the building; my men circulate the hotel 24/7. So of course they gon' notice a damn Uber driver and his passenger in a parked car just randomly sitting there," he informed her in an amused tone. "Get yo' ass the fuck out the car and up here. Now." Then he ended the call.

"So what are we doing here?" the driver questioned her while looking through his rear view mirror.

"I'm staying. How much extra do I owe you?" Naomi asked.

"Are you sure? Is everything okay?" he responded.

"Yea I'm sure, and everything is fine. Now how much do I owe you?" Naomi asked quickly ending the conversation.

Ten minutes later, Naomi found herself shyly knocking on his hotel door. When the chestnut door swung open, she had to compose herself from not fainting with too much lust.

Marquise was in nothing but a white towel. Those hard muscles already calling her name and those mesmerizing hazel eyes already beginning to eye fuck her up and down.

She looked up at his tall frame towering over her, as he began moving closer to her. Naomi reckoned he was going to kiss her but instead, he pulled her into his penthouse suite and shut the door behind her.

She felt her back hit the smooth, cold door and before she knew it he was tugging her trench coat off her body, eager to see what was underneath it.

"Damn, look at that body," he complimented her, once her trench coat had fallen to the floor. His main goal was to see what she was hiding but now that he had seen it, he couldn't control the way his dick was growing with excitement because of her. His eyes couldn't stop exploring her body.

Her lingerie was only bound to give him a heart attack. A strapless black lace bra and matching panties was what she wore underneath her coat. Absolutely nothing else. And those black louboutins looked so sexy on her feet to Marquise. He definitely couldn't wait to fuck her in nothing but her heels on.

"Who the hell told yo' sexy ass to come dressed like that?" he questioned her sternly, moving his lips to the side of her neck.

"I'd thought you like it," she responded in a soft whisper, enjoying the feel of his lips moving on her neck.

"You thought I'd like it, huh?" he queried cockily, planting sweet kisses up her neck. "I'd tell you what I don't like though..." His tone suddenly changed from gentle to tense and Naomi swore she felt a sharp bite on her ear lobe, which only increased her horny state further. "... You hidin' in yo' car away from me."

He lifted his head from the side of her neck and glared down at her with nothing but lust filled in his eyes. "You ain't think I'd forget that, now did you?

"Marquise, I just didn't think tonight was gonna be a good night," she said gently.

"But you came here half naked to see me?" he asked with a toothy smile, moving his hand down her bare waist. "How the hell you gon' come here lookin' so fucking sexy and think tonight wasn't gon' be a good night?"

"I don't know," she lied. "But I've changed my mind. All I want right now is you." Her hands moved to the front of his towel and slowly began to unroll his towel open. When it was finally opened and dropped down to the floor, Naomi smiled with delight at how aroused he was because of her. Their night hadn't even fully begun but he was so hyped up and ready to go, by the looks of things.

However, when she reached for his dick, he quickly stopped her with a quick grip to her hand.

She looked up at him with confused eyes.

"Turn around," he ordered. She quickly did as he asked and turned around for him. Then she felt his warm hand gently moving over her butt, making her smile.

"Move it for me."

Again she did as he wanted, moving her ass just for him. The more she moved it, the more his dick grew with desire for her.

"Bend it ova," he commanded lustfully, stepping back to give her space to do as he wanted. Again, Naomi obeyed making her knees touch her elbows as she bent her ass over so Marquise could get a nice, lovely view of it.

What he did next changed the entire course of Naomi's weekend. He told her to get back up and turn around to face him. Once they were eye to eye he told her straight that he wasn't letting her leave him tonight. She wasn't leaving until Sunday. She was spending the whole weekend with him and he wasn't taking no for an answer.

Even when she disagreed and said no, he didn't bother listening. He just ripped her panties off her body and lifted her legs around his torso. And then he fucked her. Fucked her into saying yes into staying with him for the weekend and fucked her into promising not to hide away from him again.

"You promise?"

"Marq... Uhh, I can't stay," she gasped, as he quickly thrusted his long length deeper into her. His long fingers dug into her ass cheeks, pushing himself fully inside her.

"You... Can't... Stay... Or... You... Won't?" he groaned, pushing himself in and out of her, between every panted word. "You stayin' Nic. End of."

He held onto her ass even tighter, thrusting his hips with force into her wet pussy. If dicks could kill, Naomi knew she would be one dead lady already.

"Marquise, fuck!" she moaned loudly. He was driving her insane. He buried his face in her neck and breathed heavily against her skin and used more force to slam his massive dick into her drenched pussy. "Yes baby... fuck my pussy, just like that... Uh!" Her head was spinning. All she could feel was Marquise fucking her, faster and faster.

"You stayin' wit' me till Sunday a'ight?" he said as he gently kissed her throat, squeezing his strong biceps around her curvy waist, as he fucked her brains out.

Naomi couldn't even really speak. This moment right now, was mind blowing. He was doing her so well against the door. She couldn't deny it.

She moaned softly, as Marquise continued to thrust deeper and harder. Her nails were digging into his muscular back and she had to wrap her thighs around his torso tighter to keep from having his dick slip out her wet pussy.

"Answer me Nicole," he groaned deeply against her neck. "Tell daddy what he wants to hear."

"I'm staying with you," she whispered breathlessly. "I promise."

She looked up only to see those hazel eyes staring down at her with happiness and when she felt her climax coming, he quickly pulled out from her pussy.

"I ain't 'bout to nut in you raw, baby girl," he explained. "And if I let you cum on my dick now, I won't be able to stop myself."

She sighed deeply, still turned on and ready for more.

"Get yo' sexy ass in the shower," he instructed with a hard spank to her soft butt. "I'll be there in a sec baby."

And just like that she obeyed, unable to break out of his authoritative spell. He was so demanding, dominating and Naomi was loving every second of it. All of a sudden she was didn't want their time together to ever end.

***

Naomi had managed to lie quickly to Tyree and told him that she was spending the weekend with Erin as Erin's cat had died. He bought it.

Erin didn't even own a damn cat! Naomi couldn't help but chuckle lightly when Marquise gently pecked her lips and reached for the whipped cream bottle again.

"Why you laughin' baby?" he queried with an arched brow and uncapped the bottle with a flick of his finger.

It was only Saturday morning and Naomi loved how she hadn't left his bed since she had come. The only times she left was to pee or to tease and fuck Marquise in the shower. But other than that, she hadn't left for anything else.

Marquise was the only who left the bed as he had made her breakfast in bed, left to collect more Magnums from the room service boy as they had run out last night, and ordered more treats for them to eat and use.

From strawberries, cherries, melted chocolate to cold whipped cream, Naomi had been kept up all hours of the night because of Marquise's talent of placing treats in places on her body where he could lick and eat it all off all at the same damn time.

Now he was just being a very bad boy. "You know how many times we used the cream already Marq?"

"I kno'. But I wanna use it again," he said with a happy smile. "I kno' you like me usin' it too." He quickly climbed on top of her and spread her legs open so he could settle between her.

Naomi looked up at him with shy eyes and down to the can in his left hand. "Why you gettin' all shy on me freaky girl?"

"I'm not Marq," she voiced gently, moving her hands to stroke his muscular biceps.

"You sure? You good?"

"I'm good," she promised with a smirk before lifting her head up to brand their lips together. The kiss was sweet and seductive and as their tongues danced together, Naomi felt the cold cream hit her nipples.

She instantly whimpered between the kiss at the cold substance, and Marquise slowly broke their lips apart before looking down at her now cream covered nipples.

Then he began to suck. Sucked like his life depended on it, with both of those hazel eyes watching the looks of pleasure sweep across her pretty face. As he sucked the cream off her left nipple, his fingers began creeping down below to her pussy and once reaching her clit, he gently began to stoke her.

"Shit, Marq," she moaned passionately watching him as he moved to her right nipple and swirled his tongue on it, teasing it to complete hardness. "Baby..."

"You like that shit, ma'?"

She nodded quickly and observed as Marquise kissed down her flat stomach, reached the top of her pussy and began planting sweet kisses on it.

It was only after ten seconds after closing her eyes when Naomi suddenly felt the cold cream hit her clit.

"Oooooo!" Her body jerked up in surprise and her eyes flew open only to see Marquise looking straight at her with a sexy smile. Those pearly white teeth were gleaming at her.

"Relax baby," he whispered, kissing her warm inner thighs before digging right in.

The touch of his tongue felt amazing on her pussy and with the way he was sucking all the cream off, Naomi swore she was in heaven.

***

"So you a teacher?"

Naomi nodded as she gently stroked Marquise's bare chest.

"Wow, that's pretty dope," he complimented her sweetly. "You are certainly one sexy ass teacher."

She laughed lightly before responding, "Thank you."

"You welcome bae," he stated, as he gently stroked her bare back. "When can I get some private lessons?"

"Private lessons?" she asked with a scoff. "You already getting all your private lessons as we speak."

"What if I want more?"

"Then it'll cost you," she confidently replied.

"Cost me?" he queried cockily, turning Naomi onto her back so he was towering over her. "You tryna rob all my money woman?"

Naomi bit her lips nervously before saying, "Maybe. You seem like you have a lot. If you want private lessons baby, you gonna have to pay me my dues."

"You already gettin' this bomb ass dick baby, that should be enough dues," he answered with a smirk, pressing his naked body closer against hers.

"But you're rich right?"

"How you kno' girl?" he questioned her curiously, with a smooth lick of his thick lips.

"You own one of the biggest clubs in Atlanta... Four seasons... You must be rich," she explained with a smile. "What do you do for a living?"

The dreaded question that Marquise was hoping that never popped up had finally popped up. He didn't even understand why things were getting so deep between him and her. She was such an easy person to be with, chill with and fucking her was heaven on earth for him. They were getting to know each other better with this long weekend that he had suddenly planned. But now getting to know each other better was taking a slight turn for the worse.

"I'm a business man," he said quietly, moving off Nicole's body to lay back on his back.

"What type of business man?" she queried curiously.

"... A business man Nic," he responded simply.

"But there's different types of bus-"

He suddenly cut across her, "Drop it Nic."

His sudden tense tone had her more curious and worried about the fact that he didn't want her knowing what he really did as a career. She needed to know.

"No, I ain't gonna drop it Marquise," she snapped at him suddenly. "I want to know."

"You don't need to worry 'bout what I do girl. Why you tryna ruin shit all of a sudden? Just drop it."

"No Marquise." She wasn't backing down now. Not now that she knew that what he did for a living was a sensitive topic for him. It only made her more curious. "You either tell me right now what you do for a living, or I leave here right now and I am never coming back."

CHAPTER 10 ~ BUSINESS MAN?

"You won't do shit," he voiced sternly. "You kno' I ain't lettin' you leave me."

"No, I'm fucking serious Marquise," she barked, lifting her body off his California king-sized bed. "You either tell me right now or else I'm leaving."

"I'on who the fuck you think you talkin' to right now," he snapped angrily, watching as she tried to get out of his bed. "Nicole, yo' ass ain't fuckin' leavin'." With one hand gripping her arm, Marquise quickly stopped her from trying to leave him, only angering her.

"Let me go!" she shouted loudly.

"No," he fumed, pulling her back onto his bed, closer to him. "I ain't lettin' you go woman, so stop tryna run."

"You gonna tell me what you do for a living Marquise?"

"No! Why the fuck you keep askin' me that bullshit?"

"Alright, so let me g-"

Marquise quickly latched his lips onto hers in order to get her to be quiet. It worked but only for a short minute. Because as soon as he moved his lips from hers to the side of her neck in an attempt to seduce her, she began pestering him again.

"What the fuck do you do Marquise?" she asked angrily before pushing him away from her and finally getting away from him.

She managed to escape out his bed and began backing away from him. "If you don't tell me, I'm leaving right now."

"You ain't goin' nowhere Nic," he fumed getting up out his bed too.

Marquise stood there, watching her momentarily trying to contemplate whether he should tell her the truth or not. He wasn't ready to tell her what she wanted to hear and wasn't sure if she was prepared for the answer. Why did she have to be so damn nosey anyway? Why couldn't she just leave this shit alone and enjoy their time together?

"Nic, you don't want to kno' the answer to that question."

"Yes I do Marq! Now tell me or I swear I am walking out of that door and you will never hear from me again!"

Marquise sighed while staring her in the eyes.

"I'm a business man, but not yo' typical one. I made all of my money from sellin' drugs and I used it to invest in my businesses."

He continued to watch her as she stood there motionless.

"I don't do it alone either, that's why it's important that I never tell anyone."

Still Naomi said nothing which only began to make him worry.

"Nic, please say something!"

Marquise watched as Naomi walked over to the bed and sat down.

"Tell me everything. I need to know and I need to understand why," she said in a gentle whisper.

Marquise walked towards Naomi and sat down beside her on the bed.

"And if I do tell you, do you promise not to leave?"

"Yes. Now tell me."

***

Naomi listened while Marquise told her everything she wanted to know which was way more than she had expected. Marquise told her about the Knight Nation, including his best friends, Blaze and Kareem and what everyone's role was within the organization, leaving her reeling from it all. Blaze was the boss and Kareem and Marquise were his right hand men. Together they owned one of the biggest and greatest drug cartels in the entire city of Atlanta.

A drug dealer? Really, you're having an affair with a drug dealer Naomi?

She had to admit that she respected him for telling her the truth just as she'd asked, and promised not tell anyone. She was the first person to admit that everyone had secrets including her. How could she really judge him knowing that what she was doing was way worse than his secret? Marquise was sleeping with a married woman with two kids, and had no idea. He didn't even know her real name for God's sake!

"Now tell me about your life. I want to know everything about you," he requested sweetly, moving his hand to stroke her cheek.

Naomi froze when he asked her. She contemplated telling him the truth after he poured out his heart and against his better judgement, told her about his life. She really wanted to be honest with Marq, but how could she after all this time had passed? Would he be as accepting as she had been? Naomi quickly decided against it and chose to continue sticking to her lie. She would tell him later and didn't want to ruin their time together any further than she already had.

"What is there for me to tell? I'm a teacher and an only child. I really don't hang out that much and I don't have a lot of friends. I have one best friend named Erin. You've already met her."

Marquise eyed her suspiciously and she tried her best to keep a straight face. She didn't want him to know that she was telling him a bold face lie.

"So you a good girl ma?" he asked with an arched brow.

"Yea I am," she responded with a shy smile.

"So anyone kno' you fuck with a thug ass nigga like me?" his lips curled into a sexy smirk.

"No."

"So nobody kno' I got you doin' bad shit ma? Nobody kno' how good I make you feel?"

Naomi smirked and said, "Nope."

"Do you crave this dick ma?"

Marquise quickly grabbed her and sat her on his lap. She straddled him and kissed his soft lips while he gripped her ass. Every ounce of self-doubt that plagued her was gone with just one kiss from him. How could this man know exactly what her body needed when she needed it?

"Tell me Nic! I need to hear you say it."

Marquise inserted himself inside of her as he kissed her neck and pinched her nipple. Naomi rode him like never before, while working her hips and becoming completely lost in him. She was addicted to his touch, to his kiss, and to this feeling that overcame her whenever he was near.

"Yes I crave you... I'm addicted to you Marq!"

Yes, she was addicted to her thug and she was going to keep him around no matter what she had to do. There was no going back now.

***

Marquise and Naomi stayed locked in that room for the remainder of the weekend, touching and teasing like two horny teenagers who just had to have each other. She was dreading returning to her normal life where Marquise didn't exist, but she had to go home to her family at some point, right? She made sure to clean every inch of her body before leaving the hotel room. She almost scrubbed her skin raw to ensure that Tyree didn't notice anything different, but that was a price she was willing to pay considering she was playing with fire. She was even able to reply to texts from Tyree when he inquired about Erin and how she was doing, while Marquise conducted official business.

"When am I gon' see you again Nicole?"

"Soon, I promise, but I have to go. I have work tomorrow and I have to get my lesson plan ready."

"You better not try to hide from me again. Don't make me come lookin' for yo' ass!"

"I won't...I promise."

Naomi kissed Marquise goodbye and he closed the car door before her Uber driver pulled off. She turned to watch as he stood there watching her drive away. She blew him a kiss and couldn't help but feel like a piece of her was missing. Seeing his handsome face drift away from her was only starting to make her sad. Naomi changed her mind about going straight home and requested that the cab driver take her to Erin's house.

Naomi: *"You home?"*
Erin: *"Yea wasup?"*
Naomi: *"OMW. Got stuff to tell you!"*
Erin: *"K... I got wine."*
Naomi: *"Good."*

Naomi was consumed in her thoughts during her entire cab ride. She didn't want to tell Erin, but she needed her advice on this entire situation. His words about what he really did for a living haunted her, and she desperately needed to make sense of it all. The only person that she could confide in was Erin and she was just going to have to woman up and do just that.

"We're here," the driver said snapping her out of her train of thought.

"Oh, thank you," Naomi said as she grabbed her purse and exited the car.

Before she could make it to the door, it was open and Erin was standing there with a glass of their favorite red wine in her hand.

"Damn, what took you so long? I need to know the tea now!" Erin said as she stepped inside her home. Naomi followed closely behind and closed the door once she was all in.

"Okay, but first, do you have some clothes I can borrow?" Naomi asked.

"Sure, you know where everything is. I ordered pizza and it should be here any minute now," Erin responded.

Naomi went down the hall to Erin's bedroom where she searched through her drawers and grabbed a pair of jogging pants and a tank top. She only had the sexy underwear she wore before, so she decided to go without any. She then stuffed the lingerie in her purse before pulling her wild curls back into a pony tail. Once she was comfortable with her appearance, she walked back down the hallway to find Erin sitting on the couch sipping wine. Naomi set her purse on the counter, picked up her glass, and took a seat next to her best friend.

"Erin, what if I told you I did something really, really bad?" Naomi asked before taking a huge gulp of wine.

"How bad? Like go Winonna Rider bad?" Erin laughed.

"No, not bad in that way, but still terrible," Naomi admitted before finishing her glass of wine.

"Girl just tell me, damn! I'm sure it's really not that bad," Erin demanded.

"I've been having an affair," Naomi blurted out.

A stunned Erin sat there with her mouth hanging open momentarily. She then stood up and went to the kitchen before returning with the entire bottle of wine. She refilled their glasses and said, "Tell me everything."

Naomi went on to explain everything that happened between her and Marquise from the moment they met up until today.

"You lying little whore. I should have known something was wrong when we saw him at that restaurant!" Erin stated.

"I know Erin and I wanted to tell you. I just didn't know how," Naomi admitted.

"Girl, don't ever be afraid to tell me anything. I'm your friend no matter what, even when you have been being a little slut," Erin laughed while Naomi slapped her arm.

"Erin seriously, I don't know what I'm going to do," Naomi said as she clutched a pillow.

"Naomi, you don't have to figure it all out today sweetie. Yes, you made a mistake, but you're not gonna do it again, right?" Erin asked.

When Naomi didn't respond, she looked at her and asked again, "Right?" Naomi kept silent.

"Naomi! You are seriously playing with fire right now! You and I both know you cannot have your cake and eat it too, especially when neither of them knows what's going on. Eventually someone is going to find out. Atlanta is only so big girl," Erin admitted.

"I know," Naomi said.

"Naomi do you love Tyree?" Erin asked.

"Yes, of course I love my husband," Naomi declared.

"Do you love Marquise?" Erin questioned.

"I don't know... I mean, I haven't even known him that long. I can't possibly love him, right?" Naomi asked.

"Girl love doesn't have a time frame, date, or stamp. When you know it you feel it in here," Erin said as she placed her hand over Naomi's heart. "But whatever conclusion you come to you are going to have to choose between the two of them before shit hits the fan. This type of shit will get you on an episode of *The First 48!*" Erin laughed.

Naomi had to laugh too. Even though Erin had a weird way of giving her advice, she knew in her heart that she was telling the truth. She was going to have to make a decision or this thing was going to end badly. All she knew was she didn't have to decide anything today and for that, she was grateful.

"Now tell me, does Mr. Biggs have an equally handsome and rich brother for me? Cuz I'll gladly take all of him and his access baggage! Just saying," Erin said as they both began to laugh. Suddenly Erin's doorbell loudly rang.

"That's the pizza. I don't know about you, but I'm starving!" Erin said as she moved to get the pizza from the door.

Images of Marquise feeding her chocolate dipped strawberries before letting little droplets of chocolate fall on her breasts and then licking them off, flooded her brain. Her body shuddered at the thought and as if he was reading her mind, a text came through.

Marquise: *"I miss you already baby."*

Naomi: *"I miss you too."*
Marquise: *"I can't get you out my head ma."*
Naomi: *"Me either."*
Marquise: *"I'm fallin' for u ma'."*
Naomi: *"I'm falling for u 2."*

Naomi couldn't believe she'd just typed those words. Hell, she couldn't believe she just admitted it to herself. The least she could do was be honest about her feelings, right? Or at least that's the lie she told herself to accept the fact that what was done was done. She sighed as she came to the realization that she'd developed feelings for Marquise that she could no longer deny. Shit had just gotten real.

CHAPTER 11 ~ FAMILY

"I'm falling for you 2."

Marquise felt his whole body light up with happiness at her response. Now all he wanted was to see her pretty face again and spend the rest of his week with her. Unfortunately, he couldn't.

Before he knew it, Monday was here and work was back on. Even though he had to focus on the business, he couldn't stop thinking about Nicole.

Nicole.

Next time he saw her, he needed to know her surname, more about her family, her goals and plans for the future. He wanted to find out everything about her. She seemed a bit closed off when it came to telling him about herself, but he figured that she just wasn't that comfortable yet around him. But he would make her comfortable as they spent more time together. She was one bad ass chick that he knew he was getting serious about. He was seriously falling for her.

At the moment, things were tense at the Knight Nation. Their archenemy and rival, Leek Carter had attacked one of their trap houses up north. He has purposely started trouble and for that, Marquise knew he had to die.

"That dumb nigga Leek thinks he's getting away with this shit. He must not fully know who the fuckin' Knight Nation are," Marquise commented with a smirk. "We got eyes everywhere lookin' for this fool. He's bound to be found soon."

"We need to find him sooner than later. He's been sellin' our shit on the streets. Our shit that he stole! We can't let him get away with this," Kareem responded, his voice filled with nothing but determination and slight anger.

"Boys... don't sweat," Blaze assured his boys. "Like Marq jus' said, we've got eyes lookin' for this fool everywhere. And when we find him... he's a dead man."

Kareem and Marquise nodded at him in agreement, before focusing on the numerous medium-sized packages lined up in front of them. "How much you think this shit is B'?"

"Probably over four hunnid pounds... Connect said he wanted us to shift double the weight, this month," Blaze responded to Kareem, as he lifted one of the brown covered parcels up and slowly teared off the paper to examine the contents. Blaze stared down at the large weight of white powder in his hands. "It's gon' be a lot of work, but we gon' get it done."

"I'll call some of the guys in a bit to come start pickin' this shit up," Kareem announced.

"Sounds like a plan," Marq replied with a grin before adding, "Speakin' of some shit... Yo B', what's up with you and Masika?" He had noticed that their relationship seemed a bit dead and he hadn't seen Masika with Blaze for a while now.

Blaze rolled his eyes in annoyance before deciding to speak. "Apparently this bitch has a son with Leek."

"What?!"

"Apparently?" Marquise questioned suspiciously. "So you ain't sure?"

"I'm not a hundred percent sure but I have a feelin' it's true."

"So are you still with her?" Kareem queried curiously.

"Not really. I mean, after findin' out that shit and realizing that she's been keepin' this away for two years kinda made me think, fuck her. So I've been vibin' with this new chick."

"Oh word?" Kareem asked.

"Yeah... I ain't sure what it is about her, but she's really different. Different than Masika and any other chick I've been with put together. Not only is she sexy as fuck, but she's intelligent, sassy and independent. If all goes well, I think I might have to wife her ass."

ARI & MISS JENESEQUA

"Woah, you can't wife her without us meetin' her first B'," Marq declared seriously. He didn't want another Masika trying to pop up in his boy's life. "She gotta get our stamp of approval before anythin' else. We yo' brothers, and we know what's best for you. Right Reem?"

"Yeah, yeah," he said in agreement. "We don't wan' another Masika to pop up."

Blaze couldn't help but chuckle at his boys lightly before commenting, "Trust me, she's no Masika. But if yo' silly asses really wan' meet her, then cool. I'll set up somethin' soon."

"You know who else I wanna meet?" Kareem asked incredulously looking straight at Marquise.

"Who?" Blaze curiously wondered.

"Marquise's new chick," he responded with a grin, making Marquise sigh softly with a head shake.

"Who?" Marquise questioned, trying to act dumb.

"Yo' don't front with me nigga," Kareem retorted. "Blaze don't know yet... But I know. I know you got some new pussy drivin' you crazy. I saw yo' whatsapp profile fool."

During their time together, Marquise had taken a picture of Nicole sleeping on his chest while he cradled her in his arms. She looked even more beautiful to him when she slept, so he just had to take a picture. That picture ended up being his whatsapp profile picture. He was a sucker for pictures too. In his previous life he was sure that he was a photographer.

Marquise couldn't help but smirk at his boys' shyly, before running a hand across his chin.

"Yeah, I got a new chick."

"Why ain't you say anythin' nigga!?" Blaze loudly asked with a smile. "This is great news! Marquise finally on lock down."

Marquise wasn't sure why he hadn't told his boys yet. He wanted to make sure that he knew for certain that he wasn't just having a one-night stand with Nicole. Now that he knew, he felt that he could talk about her.

ADDICTED TO MY THUG

"Tell us all about her," Kareem requested and Marquise did just that.

He told his best friends everything. From the very moment they met, the first time they fucked, how she did it, how she kissed, how she tasted, what she looked like, everything. Blaze and Kareem were the only niggas who Marquise trusted enough to tell about Nicole. Marquise didn't really have any family anyway and he hated talking about them too.

Blaze and Kareem were the only family he had and that's just the way shit was.

An hour later, Blaze and Kareem had things to do outside of Knight Nation business and trying to find Leek, so Marquise decided to stay behind at their main warehouse and check up on some of their boys doing work and getting ready to sell dope on the streets tonight.

It wasn't until three hours later, when one of the boys came to inform Marquise about a woman out front trying to get in to talk to Blaze.

As soon as Blaze's name was involved, Marquise knew exactly who was out front right now. And he wasn't down for seeing her tonight.

Walking out to the front entrance only made Marq irritated that he was sorting out Blaze's baby drama mama. The nigga didn't even have a baby! All their lives, Blaze, Kareem and Marq made sure that they were always strapped up and never caught up in getting any hoes pregnant. They weren't ready for babies until they had found the one. Marquise suddenly didn't mind the idea of Nicole being the one.

"What do you want Masika?" Marquise asked her, staring up and down at her curvy figure.

As annoying as she was to him, Blaze's fiancée was one bad ass chick. She had a great body. Curvy and thick in all the right places, with big titties and a fat ass and a cute face to match. It was a shame she held so much drama, because Marquise used to believe she was the perfect fit for his boy.

"I need to see my man," she announced simply. "Can you tell him I'm here?"

"He ain't here Masika."

"What?"

"I said he ain't here," Marquise repeated with annoyance, glaring down at her. "Go home."

"So where is he at?" she quickly asked, only adding to his current frustrations.

Marquise kept silent and continued to glare down at her angrily. Why couldn't she just let it go and go the fuck away?

"I asked you a question didn't I? Where the fuck is Blaze at?" She stepped forward trying to get past him.

"Chill... And I just answered you Masika, he's not around," Marquise answered her sternly, still blocking her way as she tried to get past him. "Go home ma', I'm sure he'll call you soon."

"He's too busy fuckin' that hoe to call me or even pick up his damn phone! Marq, just please tell me where he's at," she begged desperately.

"Just go home Masika... I'll tell him to call you when I see him. But I can guarantee you he's not here. It's jus' me. Why the fuck would you even come here alone Masika? You know how dangerous it is." Marquise didn't understand why she was bothering to risk her life coming to the warehouse just to see Blaze. With the amount of rivals and enemies The Knight Nation had, they would do anything to get a higher hold over them. Even if that meant killing family or friends.

"I don't care!" she exclaimed loudly. "I need to see him. I need to talk to him... He thinks I have a son-"

"And you don't?" Marq asked her suspiciously.

"No! Whoever told him that shit is just trying to ruin what we have. Marq, please believe me..." She looked at him sincerely and he was trying to see if he could tell if she was lying or not. He couldn't.

"You sure?"

Masika nodded gently and small tears began to flow out her eyes. "Please believe me, Marq." He hated seeing girls cry. It brought him to past memories that only put him in a dark place, so seeing Masika cry only made him want to stop her, immediately.

"Don't cry ma'," he whispered softly, using his fingers to gently wipe away her tears before opening his arms out to her. "I believe you."

Masika was Blaze's fiancée for a reason, right? Even though they weren't together right now and Blaze said he was vibing with this new chick, Marquise didn't like seeing Masika sad. They used to be good friends before all this shit happened. So comforting her wasn't a crime... Was it?

***

"When can I next see you beautiful?"

Naomi sighed deeply at the sound of his deep baritone over the phone. Even with him being away from her, she still found herself falling.

"I don't know Marq..." Her words trailed off nervously as she watched Christopher and Josie playing outside in their garden. Today was her day off from teaching and Tyree had gone out running some errands.

"You must kno' baby," Marquise said seductively. "You kno' I miss that pussy and I kno' you miss this dick."

She felt herself creaming on the spot and she had to turn away from the kids to regain composure over her body. The control he had over her was insane.

"I do miss you Marquise," she whispered softly. "But I'm a busy woman."

"Too busy to come see me tonight?"

She exhaled lightly before responding, "Yeah, I gotta prepare for school tomorrow."

"But if you come over, I could help you wit' all that and cook you dinner."

Naomi smiled at his attempt to get her to come see him. But she couldn't. Using the Erin excuse was making Tyree become a little suspicious. He even called Erin personally to ask about her dead cat and she almost forgot to cover for Naomi.

"Not tonight Marq, I'm sorry."

"Hmm, I guess I jus' have to see yo' sexy ass some other time," he commented sadly. She knew he wasn't happy and for that she was upset.

"I'll make it up to you, daddy," she suddenly cooed sweetly into the phone. "I promise."

"How?" he queried curiously.

"You already know how," she stated, turning back round to see Josie and Christopher still playing.

"Nah, I don't Nic," he pushed. "Tell me."

She decided to head back into her home, so that her kids wouldn't overhear her phone conversation by accident.

Once on the comfort of her loveseat, Naomi decided to tell Marquise exactly how she was going to make it up to him.

"You know that balcony outside your penthouse window?" she questioned him lustfully, knowing he already knew exactly what she was talking about.

"What 'bout it?"

"I want you to..."

"You want me to what?"

She chuckled lightly at his persistent state before continuing, "I want you to bend me over it, hold my hands behind my back and fuck me with that big, juicy dick of yours."

"Damn Nic... You so bad," he whispered happily. "I can't wait to see yo' ass even more now."

When the night finally came for them to meet, Naomi found herself in nothing on but her silver Louboutins while Marquise stroked her ass as he bent her over his balcony.

"Marq..." she purred, sticking her ass out further, seductively glancing back at him over her shoulder. He guided his dick to her tight entrance, teasing her wet folds with the head of his smooth dick.

She moaned, sliding her palms up along the edge of the balcony as the tip of his dick teased her wet pussy. She pressed back against him, hungrily grinding against his erection.

"My pussy's ready for your big dick...please don't make me beg baby," she stated boldly.

He smoothed his free hand over her firm ass, rubbing his palm up and down her warm skin.

"You'll get it Nic, I promise," he teased back, delivering a playful slap to her cheeks. He wanted to be inside her so badly. He wanted her sweet juices covering his shaft, moaning his name while he fucked her hard. Now that she was using the pill, she didn't mind him going raw inside her. And since she wasn't having sex with Tyree that much anymore, she didn't mind at all.

He slapped her ass a little harder, rubbing his tip faster between her pussy lips. "Uhh," she whimpered softly.

He parted her legs then moved his hands to her hips, gripping them hard. He slowly pushed his length inside her, filling her up until his whole shaft disappeared into her tight slit.

"Fuck baby," she growled, feeling his entire length ease inside of her pussy.

"God damn..." he groaned deep, pulling his dick back out and slowly pushing it back in again.

He leaned down, dropping warm kisses up her spine. He wanted to give her time to adjust to his thick size before he started slamming his dick into her wet pussy.

"Are you ready for this dick?" He flicked his wet tongue over her heated skin.

"Yes... I am daddy."

Her words let him know that she was ready for him. He took a slow breath, pulling his dick out from her pussy one last time.

He dug his fingers into her hips before thrusting his length hard into her pussy.

"Uhh! Shit!" she moaned loudly, her legs shaking a bit as his dick pushed into her.

"Baby... Agh!" he groaned, tilting his head up to look at the dark night sky. He started bucking his hips, thrusting deeper inside her; his eyes tightly closed, giving into the overwhelming sensation of her tight walls clenching around his hard dick.

"Fuuck," she loudly moaned.

The hard smacking noise of their bodies colliding together loudly, sounded. He tightened his hold on her hips, rocking her body hard up and down his dick.

He groaned deep with each thrust, roughly massaging his hands against her warm skin.

"You know how to treat this pussy right baby," she announced sexily.

He could feel her arousal dripping down his legs with every pull of his dick. He was coated in her juices, plunging his dick further into her wetness. She even started squirting, much to Marquise's delight.

He moved his hand over her ass, squeezing her soft flesh before delivering another quick spank.

"Oooh baby," she moaned deeply, arching her back. Naomi loved it when he got rough with her. It kept things interesting and exciting between them, something Tyree failed to do.

He pulled back his hand again, smacking her cheeks with another hard blow. "That's right, arch it for me bae," he demanded, massaging her reddened caramel skin.

"Marq...I'm close...so close..."

He was close as well. Her wet pussy drenched his dick, making it harder for him to keep up the fight of letting go and emptying his hot release deep inside her.

He slid his hand from her hip, dipping his thick fingers between her legs, pressing down hard on her pussy. His fingers quickly rubbed over her clit as he continued pumping his dick faster into her. "Cum for me Nicole."

"Marquise... Oh my…" Her moans were uncontrollable.

"Uhh...uhhhh..." she whined, unable to form words as the pleasure intensified deep within her.

Her eyes fluttered closed in pure pleasure, and her whole body shook with sexual ecstasy. Her pussy clenched tightly then pulsed hard, releasing her hot juices all on his dick.

"Uhh..." He shuddered to the feeling of her cum coating his entire dick. He thrust a few hard pumps before stilling behind her. "Fuck!" he groaned, shaking hard as his release filled inside her. It was uncontrollable and it even made a few mini tears run out his eyes. "Uhh... Nicole, I think I love you."

She froze at his words, shocked at them but also strangely happy at them. Her mouth suddenly opened and responded back, "I think I love you too, Marquise."

CHAPTER 12 ~ LOVING HIM

Nicole, *I think I love you....*

Naomi smiled as she sat behind her desk reminiscing about all of the naughty things she'd done with Marquise. She'd been on cloud nine since they'd last seen each other and she had to admit that she missed him. They'd been texting every free moment as well as calling, when she could sneak away without Tyree being suspicious. She'd become better at hiding everything from Tyree as well as masking the feeling of guilt. Hell, the feeling of guilt was pretty much non-existent now that she'd come to terms with the decision she made. Naomi realized that she loved her husband Tyree, but she also loved her boo, Marquise.

In her heart, she knew that what she was doing was wrong, but what was a girl to do with her heart and head leading her in two totally separate directions? Besides, she was tired of being the ideal mother and woman that everyone made her out to be. She loved the rush that she got when in Marquise's arms or when his hands were all over her body. Marquise brought something out of her that she'd never truly realized was there. Marquise brought out the bad girl in her and she was ready to explore exactly how far he could make her go.

Naomi decided to stay inside during her lunch while her class was away at their daily art class. **Ding!** Her phone chimed, when a text from Marq came through. Her face lit up as she read it.

Marquise: *"Hey sexy. How's work?"*
Naomi: *"Hey handsome! It's going... how about you?"*
Marquise: *"It's going. I miss u tho ma."*
Naomi: *"I miss u more."*
Marquise: *"Impossible."*
Naomi: *"Why is that?"*

Marquise: *"Cuz trust me I know. I been thinkin bout u non stop."*

Naomi: *"Yea? What about me?"*

Instead of a reply, her phone began to ring. Naomi smiled as she answered.

"Hello?"

"Why you playing wit' me?"

Naomi chuckled. "Playin' wit' you how?"

"You know I miss my pussy ma, and I need you right now."

Naomi bit down on her bottom lip while slightly shifting in her seat. "Baby, I'm at work and my class will be back any minute now."

"Well when can I see you Nic?"

"I don't know Marq, things are getting pretty busy at work."

"Too busy for me to put my face in ya pussy? I know you like that shit so you might as well come and ride my face."

Naomi's pussy was soaking wet right now and the more Marq talked about tasting her, the hornier she got.

"So you comin' ova or what?"

"Yes. I'll meet you after work but only for a minute."

Marq smiled once he knew he'd won. "Okay Nic, I'll meet you at my place."

"Okay baby."

"Okay… I love you Nic."

"I love you too, Marq."

***

"Ah! Marq!" Naomi screamed as he shoved his dick in and out of her slick pussy. She was bent over the couch while Marquise stood behind her.

Smack! "You like that shit don't you?" Marq said while smacking Naomi's ass and grabbing a handful of her hair before pulling it.

"Yes, I love it!" Naomi yelled as she felt her orgasm quickly approaching. Marquise picked up speed which caused Naomi to arch her back further.

"Yes daddy, right there!" Naomi screamed.

"That's right Nic, cum for daddy," Marquise demanded as he desperately tried to hold on to ensure that he satisfied his woman.

Naomi came undone as her orgasm crashed hard, sending shock waves throughout her body.

"Oh my God!" Naomi screamed while her legs quivered and Marquise continued fuck her, moving faster and faster until he, too, released deep inside her.

"Fuck!" Marquise yelled as he came to a complete standstill. He was exhausted after going round for round, but he loved every minute of this. He slowly pulled out of her and turned her around to embrace her. He gently kissed her forehead, then nose and lips. Marquise stared into her eyes for a moment before pulling her close and tightly wrapping his arms around her.

"Don't leave me tonight ma," Marquise said.

"I don't want to, but I have to. I've already stayed too long," Naomi admitted.

"But, I need you right here with me," Marquise stated. "I'm gonna miss you so much…"

"Baby, I'll miss you too, but if I don't get home I'll never get up in the morning," Naomi said.

"Well before you go, can I at least feed you?" Marquise asked.

Naomi stared into his sexy hazel eyes and smiled. How could she say no when Marquise looked at her the way he did and what difference would another hour really make right?

"Okay baby," Naomi said as she kissed Marquise on the lips. He smiled and let go of her, making his way to the kitchen to begin preparing a quick meal.

"So you wan' me to show you how a thug ass nigga like me be killin' it in the kitchen?" Marquise boldly stated while washing his hands in the sink before pulling various ingredients from the cabinets and refrigerator.

"Boy please! I'll believe it when I taste it," Naomi laughed.

"Yea' aite. Don't be ova there smackin' and suckin' ya fingers either," Marquise teased causing Naomi to giggle.

"Can I ask you something?" Marquise asked.

Naomi paused knowing exactly where this conversation was going. Marquise was going to question her about all thing Nicole. She released the breath she was holding in order to avoid him becoming suspicious.

"Anything," Naomi responded.

"I want to know you Nicole. I want to know everything about you because I love you and you're mine," Marquise confessed.

"Okay, ask away," Nicole replied nervously while chewing on her bottom lip.

"What's your last name? What was your childhood like?" Marquise asked while adding ingredients to the skillet he was currently using.

Naomi contemplated lying to him about her last name, but quickly decided against it. "My last name is Evans. My childhood, well…. It was an average childhood I guess. I grew up with both of my parents who are still happily married by the way. They were always big on education and living life as a young lady should. You know, not showing too much skin and never wearing red lipstick."

Marquise glanced in her direction and smiled at her. He figured she'd grown up like the Huxtables.

"What's your favorite color?" Marquise questioned.

"Purple," Naomi smiled.

"What do you want out of life Nic? Like besides teaching and your students. But, for you in the next five years," Marquis asked.

Naomi thought carefully before answering the question. "I don't know. I've never thought that far ahead," she lied.

Marquise just shook his head as if he was etching her words into his brain. It was then that Naomi remember she was still completely naked and instantly smiled.

"What you laughin' at girl?" Marquise asked.

"Nothing baby. While you cooking I'm gonna hop in the shower," Naomi said.

"Okay, jus' don't take too long ma. You gotta eat this while it's hot, aite?" Marquise said.

"Okay baby," Naomi cooed as she sashayed completely naked to the bathroom.

"You keep doin' dat shit you gone get into some more trouble tonight girl," Marquise said.

Naomi shook her head and laughed, as she made her way into the bathroom for a steaming hot shower. She turned on the water and closed the door, allowing the steam to completely fill the bathroom. She'd told Tyree that she and another teacher were working on a project for their classes as an effort to teach the children about community service. She was amazed at how well the explanation worked considering she'd been sneaking off with Marquise more often. She was almost positive that he would call her, so she left her phone in the car on purpose. There was no way she would have been able to explain to Marquise why Tyree was calling so to keep the peace, she did what she had to do. Now Tyree was a whole other story and she knew she would have to face the music when she finally made it home.

***

Naomi entered her home as quiet as humanly possible, lightly closing the door behind her. After eating dinner with Marquise, she drank a little wine and talked for a little while before coming home. Truthfully, she was dreading this very moment and decided to stay a little longer, but once she got in her car she immediately regretted it. Tyree had called her over twenty times and texted her at least ten times, begging her to call home. She made sure she erased her call log so that her lie would work. What she wasn't prepared for was the fact that Tyree would be up waiting for her.

Naomi locked the front door and turned around to find Tyree standing right in front of her with a scowl on his face. She inwardly rolled her eyes as she prepared for the argument to begin.

"Naomi, what the fuck is wrong with you? I been calling your ass for the three hours and texting you!" Tyree yelled.

"I know you've been trying to reach me, but my phone died and was buried inside of my purse," Naomi lied.

"So you didn't think to use someone's phone to call home and check on your children? Or to check in with your husband?" Tyree questioned.

"No because I told you I'd be working late, remember? I did that hours ago and I figured the kids would be okay because they were at home with their father," Naomi defended herself.

"You know Naomi, that's bullshit and you know it! Yo' ass been going out with yo' friends and hardly spending time at home anymore. You barely even been spending time with yo' fucking kids cuz you so busy running in the damn streets! What the fuck is wrong with you?" Tyree yelled.

"Please Tyree, let's not start this shit, okay? Why is this such a big deal to you, huh? Because I been out somewhere besides home every damn day? Why, because I choose to enjoy life sometimes instead of being an old maid?" Naomi asked.

"No, because you are being a terrible wife and a bad fucking mother! These kids ask about where you are over and over all damn day! What the fuck do you think this is Naomi?" Tyree asked stepping closer in her direction. Tyree balled up his fist and his chest heaved with anger.

"Excuse you? A bad mother and a terrible wife? The last time I checked I have spent all of my damn time in this marriage being the best fucking mother and wife, while a provider for us even when you couldn't! I have done nothing but lift you up so that you could still feel like a damn man and now because I'm taking time to smell the roses, I'm such a horrible person? Fuck you, you selfish bastard!" Naomi yelled while turning around to unlock the front door that she'd just entered minutes ago.

"Where the hell do you think you going Naomi?" Tyree questioned.

"To Erin's, is that okay with you? Maybe I need to re-evaluate my life to find out why I'm such a terrible wife and bad mother! I'll be back to see my kids in the morning," Naomi said before exiting her home and making her way down the driveway to her car.

"Naomi if you leave-" Tyree threatened while following her towards her car.

"If I leave what, Tyree? What the fuck are you going to do, divorce me? Please go back inside and get some damn sleep. Whatever you do just leave me the fuck alone!" Naomi said as she hurried inside of her car, started it, and reversed out of the driveway.

CHAPTER 13 ~ CHOOSING HIM

Tears stung her eyes at the words that left her husband's mouth. One thing she'd never been was a bad mother and always had been a good wife to Tyree, even when he showed no appreciation for all of her hard work. How dare he say such things to her? Sure, she had been staying gone a little more, but she always made sure she spent ample time with her children to make up for it. Hell, she'd even been putting up with Tyree's boring ass and all of his whining, pretending to be paying attention.

Tears flowed freely as she drove towards Erin's house. She didn't bother calling considering she knew it was a school night and she'd be home. She contemplated going back to Marquise but dismissed the thought as quickly as it came to her head. There was no way he could see her this upset without explaining to him the reason behind it. She knew one thing for sure, Tyree was going to regret every hurtful word that left his mouth because she was going to make sure she became the terrible wife that he claimed she'd already become.

Naomi pulled up in front of Erin's house and quickly hopped out, while making her way to the door. She rang the doorbell and wiped her eyes while waiting for her to come to the door. She could hear the shuffling of house shoes echoing throughout the house.

"Who is it?" Erin yelled.

"Naomi," she said as Erin began to quickly take the locks off of the door.

Erin opened the door and took one look at her friend and hugged her. No words were needed as Naomi cried on her shoulder while Erin just let her be.

"Come inside, it's chilly out," Erin said as she stepped aside and Naomi walked inside. Erin closed the door and placed the locks back on the door.

Naomi moved to the couch and took a seat before Erin made her way to her and did the same. They sat in silence momentarily before Naomi had calmed herself enough to tell her friend what happened. She explained what happened and even told her all about where she'd come from before making it home.

"Oh hell no he didn't call you a bad mother! That muthafucka!" Erin stated.

"Yes that bastard did! I mean Erin, when has my life ever really been about what I want? I have never been in a position to be free and just be me without someone getting inside my head," Naomi admitted. Erin knew all too well the pressures Naomi endured from both her parents and Tyree on a daily basis.

"I know girl. He had no right to say those things to you and I understand why you're hurt," Erin admitted.

"I am sick and tired of living life the way everyone else wants me to live it! I am tired of being little miss perfect and the ultimate soccer mom while he gets off easy. I mean, how many women would still stay with a man who hasn't been able to hold down a job for three damn years?" Naomi asked.

"Hell, definitely not me bitch, you a good one, cuz his ass would have been out on the curb," Erin chimed.

"Exactly. None Erin, and he doesn't even appreciate me or all I do for our family. I want to come home to someone who truly loves me and knows me like the back of their hand. I can honestly say that Tyree doesn't really know me. He only knows the perception of me that I chose to let him believe," Naomi admitted to herself for the first time.

Yes, she'd been with her husband for years and he was all she ever knew, but she always felt that there was more out there waiting for her. She settled because that's what she'd been taught to do as a little girl and now she was regretting it. She couldn't believe that now her life was spiraling out of control and now her happily ever after had been shattered.

Naomi hadn't even noticed Erin had left the couch until she returned with two glasses full of their favorite red wine.

"Look, you know I love you and you're like a sister to me so I gotta be honest with you. You are going to have to choose where you want to be. You were happy with Tyree before because you had no idea what else was out there for you to choose from. You had no other perception of how a man should be because you'd only been with him. Now that you got a taste of that and you know the difference, things will never be the same until you choose," Erin said.

Naomi remained silent as she took a sip of wine from her glass and contemplated what her best friend was saying.

"You're not happy Naomi, and things are only going to get worse between you two if you don't do something about this. I seriously do not want to have to explain to the police why I busted Tyree's head wide open for coming at you the wrong way!" Erin yelled.

Naomi almost spat her wine out from laughing at her best friend.

"Damn girl, you done got more action in the last few months than I done had in the last few years! Hunny, yo' life needs to be a damn movie girl. I'm just saying," Erin laughed. Naomi appreciated Erin trying to cheer her up. She could always count on her best friend to be there for her without passing judgment. Erin had spoken so much truth though and Naomi knew she was right. She did have to choose and shit in her life was only going to get worse if she didn't do something soon. She had to ask herself who would she choose though. Tyree was her husband and the father of her children. How could she just abandon all of those years?

On the other hand, Marquise was everything she ever needed in a man. He was sweet, attentive, good in bed, and not to mention rich as hell. There was the fact that he had no idea that she was married or even had children. They'd never even discussed ever having a family and she just didn't know how he would feel about it.

She didn't have the answer at that very moment and she didn't know if she would tomorrow either. But what she did have was her best friend and an entire bottle of wine that she refused to let go to waste.

***

Naomi's head was still reeling from the events that took place the night before. After leaving Erin's house that morning, she drove home to find Tyree sleeping on the couch. She didn't bother to wake him, as she made her way upstairs to their bedroom to take out her work clothes for the day. She then woke up her children and made them their favorite breakfast as she did almost every morning until recently.

She had to admit she'd really missed their smiling little faces, full of excitement, and their witty remarks. She loved her kids with everything she had and no matter what Tyree thought, she was going to continue to be the best mother she knew how to be. After feeding them and cleaning the kitchen, she got dressed for work. She was out the door without even saying a single word to Tyree.

All day Erin's questions plagued her. She hadn't been able to focus all day and her class was beginning to notice. She tried her best to shake off the feeling of despair that came over her, but she just couldn't get her head together. During class, there was a soft knock on the door and Naomi went to answer it. At the door was the secretary from the office Mrs. Jefferson.

"Mrs. Evans, you have a delivery at the front desk," she said.

"A delivery? Are you sure it's for me?" Naomi asked with a confused expression on her face.

"Yes, I'm positive," she said.

"Well, can you just put it to the side for me?" Naomi asked.

"Well um, it's taking up quite a bit of space and the principal is asking that you come to see what it is," Mrs. Jefferson explained.

Naomi was completely confused as to what in the hell she was referring to. "Ok, well can you keep an eye on my class for me while I go see?" she asked.

"Of course," Mrs. Jefferson said.

Naomi exited her classroom and made her way to the main office. She turned the corner and stopped in her tracks. Her mouth fell open at the sight in front of her and instantly felt tears sprang to her eyes. Inside of the office were, two dozen long-stemmed roses with a note attached. She tore the note off and read:

Ms. Evans,

You are an amazing teacher and an even better human being. No good deed goes unseen and because of that you will forever be rewarded.

Love,

M

Naomi wiped away the tears that threatened to fall as she noticed five large boxes sitting in the middle of the floor. Naomi bent down to open one of the boxes and smiled at its contents. Inside were tons of school supplies, toys, snacks, and even decorations. She opened each box before calling the principal and requesting that someone help her put the boxes away. She was going to make sure that these things went to good use and that each child within the school enjoyed every moment.

Once again Marquise managed to show her all of the reasons why she should choose him. Never had Tyree surprised her at work and barely bought her flowers throughout the course of their relationship. He'd never gone the extra mile to make her smile or make her feel appreciated. Marquise was definitely winning in her book and she was going to make sure he was rewarded for his good behavior. Oh how she couldn't wait to thank him properly.

CHAPTER 14 ~ NEW IDEAS

Her hands travelled up his warm muscular chest, slowly feeling every aspect of his hot body.

Three days.

Three days they had gone without having sexual intercourse. Three days. Three days and Naomi's pussy was dying for some special attention. Between work and arguing with Tyree all the damn time, Naomi had been so busy. And with Marq running the streets with his boys, he had been busy too. Three days though without getting some from her boo? Lord knows she had been going insane. Her sex toys weren't helping. They were not as big or good as Marquise Lewis.

Her hands slowly travelled back down his chest. She was trying to get to the big treasure that she hadn't had in three days.

Three days, three hours and twenty-five minutes.

Yes, she had been counting nonstop.

Once she had reached her treasure, she began to stroke it. Slowly, up and down she stroked. As she stroked he groaned, telling her that she was doing everything right. His dick immediately began to grow bigger by the minute.

"Nicole..." He groaned her name as she continued to play with him, knowing that soon he would want things to go further.

She said nothing. Instead, she leaned into Marquise's neck and started licking him, knowing that it would drive him insane.

Three days. Three days way too long.

It didn't take long for Naomi's top to be off her body, or her bra, or her shorts. And it certainly didn't take long for Marquise's pants to be pushed down to his ankles.

"Turn around," he whispered in her ear and she did as he asked. She turned, laid on her side and slightly bent her knees, slightly poking her butt out towards him.

His hard body pressed up behind her. She felt his hands tug down her black thong and his hands spread apart her ass cheeks as he pushed himself into her tight pussy hole.

"Shit...Marq." Her gentle moans couldn't be stopped even if she tried. His fingers tightened around her sides, pushing his length deeper between her tightness.

"Fuck," he groaned as he rocked his hips into her firm ass, his bed dipping under the shifting weight of their bodies, as he thrust his dick inside her pussy.

"Damn..." She sighed quickly the more he filled her upright.

Three days.

Every hard inch of his big dick was buried deep between her legs. She spread her legs a little further to give him more room to move.

Three days too long.

She moaned softly when he started rocking back and forth slowly, allowing her to feel each hard ridge of his dick.

"Marq...that feels so fucking good," she groaned, tilting her hips a little higher so he could push deeper into her pussy.

He dug his fingertips deeper into her sides, forcefully pulling her hips back against his. "Fuck, Nic... Baby," he groaned.

The harder he went into her, the better it felt.

His hands reached underneath her, wrapping his long fingers around her hard breasts, leaning into her back.

"So nice and tight..." he groaned, squeezing her nipples between his fingers. A soft sigh escaped her when he leaned closer, cupping her breasts in his hands and giving them a firm squeeze.

She couldn't help but feel happy hearing his groans get louder and louder by the second. He started increasing the force and speed in his thrusts, rocking her body harder against his.

Her firm ass cheeks roughly hit against his hips, creaking the bed springs underneath them. She moaned deep in her throat with each thrust of his big dick.

A small shiver raced up her spine as his warm breath blew against the back of her neck.

"You feel so good baby." She instantly blushed at the words that left his mouth.

"Three days without this pussy, you're never doing that again..." she teased, pumping her body with his powerful thrusts.

"Hmmm... definitely not," he groaned, squeezing her ass cheeks as he moved her body to meet his thrusts. "Pussy so good, make me wan' wife yo' fine ass Nic."

Naomi softly whimpered, biting her lip hard as his hand travelled down the curve of her back, resting firmly on her round ass. His hand smacked one of her soft cheeks again.

"This dick belongs to me and me only," she moaned loudly, as his dick drove harder into her slick pussy.

"You got that right...This dick only belongs to you, girl," he groaned over her. "Only you baby," he breathed warmly against her neck.

She could feel both the heavy beating of their hearts, pounding loudly in their chests.

The thick veins in his dick pulsed hard against her tight walls, making her thighs twitch as his pussy spasmed around his thrusting shaft.

She almost fell out of his arms when he thrusted deep, hitting her most sensitive spot. "Ugh! Marq, right there..." she whined, breathing heavy. The harder he rammed into her pussy, nailing her G-spot with no hesitation, she was sure he would drive her into a mind-blowing orgasm.

"Shit," he groaned, digging his fingertips into her thigh. "I love this pussy and... I love you baby..."

"I love you too Marq."

***

Hearing him say during sex how he wanted to wife her, began to make her think.

What would life be like with Marquise as her man?

She knew that she would be happy. She certainly wouldn't have to work as much as she was now and she could be a stay-at-home mom. Marquise would take care of her and their babies... right?

"So have you ever thought about having a family... Getting married?" she questioned him curiously, while moving closer deeper into his arms.

"Having a family?" he asked her back. "Yeah... Yeah... I thought 'bout it, but I ain't been focused on it."

Naomi contemplated to herself for a bit before questioning him again. "What about marriage? Do you see yourself settled down in the next couple of years?"

"Couple of years?" he queried with a light chuckle. "Nah ma'... I ain't thought that far yet. To be honest, I ain't even sure how I'm supposed to feel 'bout all that right now 'cause marriage ain't never been an option for me. I've been so used to just working hard and tryin' to get this paper."

"So you don't plan to get married one day Marq?"

"...I don't know ma'. I think I will one day... Not right now though."

* * *

"I can't wait to see you again baby. When you free next?"

Naomi stared down at the text from her boo with a weak smile.

Talking to him about marriage had made things awkward for her. It didn't help that she was married already and had kids. A small part of her wanted Marquise to be serious about marriage, so that she could be serious about leaving Tyree. Because there was no way that she was dealing with all these arguments anymore.

"So you going out again tomorrow? And coming in late too?"

Naomi looked up with a frown to see Tyree standing at the edge of their bed with his arms crossed and an angry expression locked on his face.

"And so what if I do? What's it to you?"

"I'm your husband Naomi!" he shouted in protest. "You don't even make time for me anymore! When was the last time we had sex?!"

"First of all, now you wanna be my husband?" she asked with a rude scoff. "But a few days ago I was a bad mother to my kids, right? Now you on some bullshit about how I don't make time for you. Nigga, shut UP! I'm not gonna make time for someone who clearly doesn't appreciate all I do."

"I don't appreciate all you do?"

"No you don't! Because if you did, then I wouldn't be telling you that you don't!" she exclaimed.

"You know what? I think its best I sleep on the couch tonight," Tyree retorted.

"Yes, I think its best that you do."

"Okay."

"Cool," Naomi snapped.

"Alright."

"Nigga, why you still talking? The conversation is over. Buh-bye," Naomi concluded rudely before reaching for her night lamp and turning it off.

When Tyree finally decided to leave the bedroom, Naomi reached for her iPhone and quickly texted Marquise. She would have to just figure out a way to tell Marquise the truth about her life. But she knew that day was far, far, far away for now. Some secrets were just best being left in the dark a little while longer.

"I'm free tomorrow bae."

***

Naomi rubbed her fingers in a circular motion on his chest, as she watched him just be. Marquise was sound asleep after what she'd just put on him and she honestly couldn't blame him.

She was dead tired herself, but she knew if she did fall asleep, she was going to be out for the night. She had to go to work in the morning and she couldn't allow her children to wake up without seeing her face. Once again she'd fought with Tyree, but it was all worth it because when she was in Marquise's arms, none of that bullshit mattered.

She had to admit to herself that Marquise's commitment issues frightened her. How was she going to tell him about her kids now when he wasn't sure if he even wanted to be married? How could she plan a future with someone who really didn't know what they wanted? Naomi had expectations now and if she chose him, she had to weigh all of her options. Did she choose to be with the man who she'd been loyal to for years, bore his children, and planned to spend the rest of her life with? Or did she choose the man who made her feel like no other, showed her love, and pure appreciation despite her flaws?

Naomi sighed causing Marquise to shift in his sleep and pull her closer to him until she was neatly tucked into his side. She smiled as she snuggled closer and gently kissed his neck.

"What's wrong?" Marquise asked breaking her train of thought.

"Nothing. Why do you ask?" Naomi questioned as she tried to keep her heart from racing.

"You wide awake and I know I fucked you good. You should be as tired as I am," Marquise chuckled as he kissed her forehead.

Naomi laughed, "I'm fine. Just thinking about everything I have to do tomorrow."

Marquise turned until he was facing her and propped his head up on his elbow. "Oh yea? Like what?" he asked.

Naomi was completely thrown off guard. She thought her answer would have been sufficient and now that he was asking more questions, she had to think fast to hide the real reason.

"My mind's just racing. You ever create a mental list of everything you have to do and realize that the list is too damn long?" Naomi chuckled.

Marquise smiled and continued to observe her as if he was waiting for her to say more. When she didn't offer anything else, he asked, "Is it anythin' I can help you with?"

Naomi just stared at him for a moment. She was in awe with this man and he continued to amaze her each day she spent with him.

"No baby, you've already helped enough," Naomi smiled. They continued to lay in each other's arms as if the world outside didn't exist, and that's the way Naomi preferred it to be.

CHAPTER 15 ~ TROUBLED THOUGHTS

It was a beautiful afternoon and Naomi was enjoying spending the day with her children. All week she'd been fighting with Tyree and she was grateful for the peace she was currently experiencing. Her children played in the park while she sipped her cup of coffee and smiled. They played as if they didn't have a care in the world, and she was happy for that. She didn't want her babies to know what was really going on between her and their father. Things were definitely different in the Evans' household, but her babies didn't seem to notice so that's all that really mattered to her.

Since she'd been sitting in the park, Naomi had really had some time to think about her current predicament. She'd decided that she was going to come clean with Marquise about everything. If they were going to make this thing work, he had to know the truth even if that meant he was going to be mad at her. Truth was, Naomi didn't know how he would take the news but at this point, it was becoming hard to look him in the face each day knowing she was living a lie. He deserved to know after everything he'd come clean with her about. Marquise had been an open book and she'd vowed to become the same, even if that meant losing him in the end.

"Mama, look at me!" her son screamed from the top of the slide.

"Yes big boy, I see you!" Naomi cooed as he slid down the slide, cheesing all the way. She glanced in her daughter's direction who was currently playing on the see-saw with another little girl. She was glad that she'd made a friend because being cooped up with your brother and father 24/7 could be exhausting at times. Besides, every girl needed girl time, right?

"Ding! Ding!" Her phone suddenly sang just as a text message came through.

Naomi looked down at her phone a smiled when she saw a message from Marquise.

Marquise: *"I need to see you ma."*

Naomi: *"Oh yea? You miss me?"*

Marquise: *"Girl stop playing you know I do."*

Naomi: *"You sure it ain't this pussy you missing?"*

Marquise: *"Nah, I just need to see you bae."*

Naomi: *"Lol, okay when?"*

Marquise: *"Tonite?*

Naomi: *"K"*

Naomi smiled and glanced over at her children who were still running around in the park. She sighed at the reality of it all beginning to set in. If she chose Marquise, life as they knew it was going to change forever. She was going to have to explain to them that her and daddy were not going to be together anymore. Was she really ready to alter their lives forever? Was Marquise even going to accept her babies after learning that she'd been lying to him for so long?

"Ding! Ding!" Just as the thought crossed her mind another text came through

Marquise: *"I love you Nic."*

Naomi: *"I love you more, Marq."*

Naomi couldn't help but smile from the confirmation she felt in her gut. Her mind told her to continue to wait, but her heart refused to live a lie any longer. Either they were going to give it their all or nothing at all. In the meantime, she needed to come up with a game plan on exactly how she was going to tell him. She quickly realized that after she told him this there was no going back, and she was going to have to come clean with Tyree as well. Now how in the hell was she going to tell her husband that she was having an affair, was the real question.

*** *

"Nic? Why haven't I been to yo' crib?" Marquise asked while they were eating dinner.

Naomi looked up from her plate and stared at him momentarily. Now how in the hell was she going to answer this question? She was taking her time with telling him what was going on, but when he asked her things like this she just didn't know what to say.

Just tell him girl! she thought to herself. "My house is being remodeled," Naomi lied before she had the chance to think it through.

Fuck! Another lie? she said to herself as she went back to eating her food. She was purposely avoiding eye contact because she was almost positive that if he made eye contact he would know he would know she was telling him a bold face lie.

"Remodeled huh? Who you got doin' the work?" Marquise asked as he shoveled more food into his mouth.

"Uh, just a contractor that Erin recommended to me after he did some work for her last year," Naomi responded.

"Well what's the name of the company? You gotta be careful with this type of shit, ma'. Niggas will take full advantage of a beautiful single woman that don't kno' no betta," Marquise admitted.

"Smith and Son I think. His name is Darryl," Naomi lied as she felt her heart beating a mile a minute. She was almost positive that sweat was forming on her nose and brow, but she still made sure she made eye contact.

Marquise eyed her suspiciously and replied, "Well how long he been on the job? I can come by and check shit out if you wan'."

"No! It's fine really, and I trust him to deliver when he said he would. I kind of got behind with my payments so that delayed the process a little," Naomi said almost too eagerly.

"Nic, why didn't you just say that? You know whateva you need I got'chu, just say the word, aite? I'm ya' man, that's what I'm here for," Marquise declared.

Naomi smiled. "I know you would baby, and I really appreciate it. I'm just not use to being able to depend on anyone when it comes to my finances," she admitted truthfully.

"Well get used to having a real nigga around," Marquise smiled, as they both continued to eat. Naomi sipped her wine as she zoned out, contemplating her next move. She was positive that this was going to come up in conversation again and it would be best to tell him the truth now rather than find out for himself.

"Baby, did I tell you 'bout my brother's girl?" Marquise asked totally snapping her out of her thought induced trans.

"Uh, no you didn't. Is everything okay?" Naomi questioned.

"He just found out she's been lying to him and got a kid. A fuckin' kid she been hidin' from him for years!" Marquise declared.

Naomi felt as if the wind had been knocked out of her. Was he serious or was he on to her? She was sitting there with her mouth hanging wide open and unsure of how she should respond.

"Fucked up right? She says the shit ain't true, but he swears it ain't no lie. I mean who the fuck denies they kid to be with somebody?" Marquise stated.

Okay I'm confused now.... Is he talking about me or not?

"So did you talk to him about it?" Naomi nervously asked while picking at her food.

"Yea', we talked 'bout it at first and we agree it's fucked up. He said he ain't fuckin' wit' ha ass no more," Marquise declared.

Naomi remained silent while she began to feel sick to her stomach.

"All I know is I'd go crazy if that shit happened to me, real talk," Marquise admitted firmly.

"Yeah I bet," Naomi said as she shoved more food into her mouth. She was guilty as fuck and almost thought she'd been caught red handed. If she told him now, he would be disgusted with her and probably leave her alone for good. See, the problem was she just wasn't willing to take that chance because she was too far gone. She was so in love with this man and losing him would devastate her. She knew she had to tell him eventually, but today just wasn't the day.

Naomi pretended to listen as he went on and on about the situation. Her stomach was rolling and she felt as if she was going to pass out. Sweat was forming on her brow and she was in desperate need of some air.

"Baby, you a'ight?" Marquise said as he scooted his seat back, stood up, and began walking towards her.

"Uh yea I think so," Naomi lied.

"Are you sure? You look a little pale," Marquise questioned as he placed his hand on her forehead as if he was checking her for a fever.

"Honestly, I'm not. I feel like I'm coming down with something," Naomi lied.

"Nic, why didn't you say somethin' earlier? I wouldn't have asked to see you if I knew you were sick," Marquise said as he wiped sweat from the bridge of her nose.

"I know Marq, I just wanted to see you," Naomi said.

Marquise smiled as he stared into her eyes before gently kissing her on the forehead.

"Let me take care of you," Marquise offered sweetly.

"No, that's okay, really, I will be just fine. I just need to go home and get in bed, that's all," Naomi declared.

Marquise stared at her momentarily. "Are you sure Nic? It's okay, I really I wan' to take care of you, ma'," he said.

"Really baby, it's fine. You already stuffed me with a delicious meal. I'll just go home and dope myself up so that I can feel better for school tomorrow," she said with a smile.

"Okay Nic. Yo' ass so stubborn but okay, if you say so," Marquise said as he grabbed her purse from the counter and pulled her seat back. They walked out of the door and stepped onto the elevator that took them down to the first floor. Marquise wrapped his arms around her and kissed the top of her head just as the doors opened on the first floor. They exited the building stepping into the cool air of the night. Marquise walked her to her car and opened the car door before she slid inside. Naomi started her car and looked up into his eyes.

"Call me if you need anything Nic, I mean it," Marquise demanded.

"I promise I will if I do," Naomi said as she tugged on his shirt and kissed him gently on the lips.

"I love you Nic," Marquise said.

"I love you more," Naomi said before he closed the door. She put her car in drive and exited the parking area.

Naomi breathed a huge sigh of relief as she hopped on the expressway. She didn't know how or when she'd become so good at lying, but mentally patted herself on the back. Erin's words played in her head: *Girl, these men lie all the damn time to get what they want and don't give two fucks who they hurt in the process. Why can't we have our cake and eat it too?* Even though Erin was trying to be a good friend by making her feel better about what she was doing, she still knew she was foul.

Tonight Marquise made it extremely hard for her to be completely honest with him. She'd planned on coming clean about everything until he started asking questions. Then the bombshell he dropped on her about his brother Blaze and his girl, only made matters worse. He'd told her exactly what he would do if it were him, and now that she knew that it made it virtually impossible for him to tell her the complete truth. Would he really leave her alone and just throw away what they have, or would he be more understanding if it were actually him in those shoes?

Whatever it was, she wasn't going to find out tonight. Naomi was going to have to find out another way to tell him everything and a way to make him stay in the process. She wasn't ready to forget everything that they shared and she definitely wasn't ready to never feel his hard body between her legs ever again. As far as she was concerned, Marquise was hers and only hers. She was going to do everything in her power to keep it that way, no matter what lies she had to tell. But for now, she had to get her head together for the bigger battle she was going to face once she got him. Tyree was going to want to argue and she just wasn't in the mood to deal with his shit right now.

CHAPTER 16 ~ FIXING IT

"Naomi, I said we need to see a counselor!" Tyree yelled. She sighed while listening to him rant once again. It had been two whole days since she'd seen Marquise because she was almost positive that if she walked out of that door, Tyree was going to follow her. She was going to have to be smarter about what she was doing from now on, even if that meant starting fights to make him avoid her. She was becoming more and more turned off by him. Her tolerance level for his bullshit was at an all-time low and frankly, she didn't care about how he felt.

"Naomi, I'm serious! If you don't come to counselling I want a divorce!" Tyree said as he blocked the doorway to their bedroom with his arms folded over his chest.

"Oh yea'? Well get them fucking papers ready nigga, cuz I ain't going!" Naomi declared.

"So you just ready to throw this all away? Look me in the eyes and tell me," Tyree demanded. "You don't want to fix our marriage?"

"Nigga, you the one making idle threats, not me! You not giving me no other option but counselling. I don't think that's going to help us and our marriage!" Naomi stated. "Counselling ain't gonna help fix it!"

"Well what is going to help us Naomi? You're barely home and we don't even have sex anymore. We used to be friends and right now it seems like we are enemies. I don't know what else to fucking do!" Tyree said.

"Well for one you can stop nagging me all the time Tyree! Stop being on my damn back and stop getting on my case about everything I do or where the hell I go! Be the damn man in this marriage for a change! Go and get a fucking job!" Naomi yelled.

Tyree glared at her with balled up fists as he allowed her words to sink in. Tears filled his eyes as Naomi continued to stand in front of him with her hands on her hips and an unfazed expression on her face. She didn't care about his feelings and it was becoming more apparent with each passing day. He was beyond hurt and didn't understand what had happened to the loving wife he once knew.

***

"And I don't know want to do. Maybe you could talk to her for me?"

Erin stared plainly at Tyree before taking a small sip of her coffee again. Why had she even agreed to come out and meet this fool? This fool that did nothing for her best friend.

"Yeah I'll talk to her," she lied effortlessly, knowing that the only talking she would be doing with her best friend would be to find out about the bomb ass sex she was having with her new rich boo.

Tyree was a fool. A fool that Erin couldn't stand to see her best friend with. She hated him. Despised everything about him. The fact that he couldn't provide for his family like a man was supposed to and take care of his kids - it made her sick.

So to find out that Naomi was shacking up with someone new made Erin extremely happy for her best friend. All she wanted was for her to be happy. After all, she was her best friend and she cared so much about the kid.

"Thank you," Tyree responded happily. "Please just try and find out what's going on with her. I love her and I don't want to lose her anytime soon."

"I hear ya'," Erin replied simply before getting up out her seat. "I gotta leave. I have things to do."

"Okay," he said sadly. "Talk to you soon?"

"Talk to you soon."

CHAPTER 17 ~ TRUE TESTS

"So he's wit' her now?" Marquise queried curiously.

"Yeah," Kareem responded casually. "We finna do this now?"

"Yeah, we need to," Marquise stated calmly. "We gotta make sure she ain't anotha Masika and we don't wan' her causin' our bro problems. Make the call. Make him think it's an emergency or somethin', that'll get him to come."

Five minutes later, Marquise listened in to Kareem's call with Blaze.

"Yo nigga," he greeted Blaze simply.

"'Sup man?"

"Where you at?"

"I'm with bae... I told you guys yesterday I'm busy today. That's why I took a day off."

"Well, you gon' need to come in now lover boy," Kareem responded, looking at Marq with a silly smirk.

"What the... Why?" Blaze queried rudely.

"Got an emergency, a 308."

"Got'cha. Usual spot, yeah?"

"Bet," Kareem concluded before ending the call.

Thirty minutes later, Blaze had arrived and Marquise and Kareem sat around the table playing cards, watching his confused facial expression.

"What the... Where's the fuckin' emergency?" Blaze questioned them both angrily. "I told yo' stupid asses I was spendin' time with my girl today and y'all just had to ru-"

Marquise cut him off with a loud chuckle before responding, "Chill B'. We told you we wanted to meet her soon. Soon is now, now."

Blaze stared at Marquise with an intrigued look before asking, "So what'chu fools finna do?"

"We wanna test her," Kareem stated simply. "You ain't gotta do shit but sit down here and play a card game with us. We've got a few of our boys comin' through any minute now who are gonna scare her up a bit."

"Scare her up how?!" Blaze questioned loudly.

"Chill," Marquise said with a soft sigh. "They jus' gonna be dressed in all black, have machetes and guns and pull up next to yo' Lambo out front. She'll think they won't see her because of the tinted windows, which she's right 'bout, but they kno' she's in there. We jus' wanna see if she's gonna have enough heart to be worried 'bout you and come thru to check up on you."

"That's one dumb motherfuckin' test," Blaze declared. "Regardless if she comes to check up on me, I'm still stayin' wit' her."

"Hey, and we ain't gon' stop you, nigga," Kareem announced. "We jus' wanna know how down she is, for our personal knowledge. A'ight?"

Blaze nodded stiffly before sauntering to the empty head center seat. Marquise watched as he picked up the upside down cards in front of him and looked at them before frowning.

"Y'all niggas are cheatin' cuz you kno' I'm the best at this game. Re-shuffle the cards," he demanded in a bossy tone.

"No nigga, we already started!" Kareem protested.

"Re-shuffle the cards fools," Blaze laughingly said, as he grabbed Kareem's cards and reached ahead to grab Marquise's.

As he reshuffled, Marquise couldn't help but think back to his brother's girl. He really wanted to meet her and hoped she came out of his car. He was hoping she wasn't one of those weak chicks that expected a male to always protect her. Sometimes a chick needed to protect her man too. He was hoping that Anika was that chick.

Ten minutes into their game, she still hadn't arrived. Even though Marquise and Kareem were sure that their plan had happened since the boys they had ordered to pull up next to Blaze's car out front had come in, taken off their masks and said that they had done what they were instructed to do.

It wasn't until twenty minutes later, Marq noticed the brown warehouse door open and gently stepping inside was a pretty, light-skinned chick with curly, thick hair that passed her curvy hips. A silver pistol was right by her side as she walked in.

"Yo Blaze... she's here!" Kareem shouted with delight.

"Damn, she got yo' gun too!" Marquise shouted.

By the look of things on her pretty face, she wasn't happy. And Marquise knew exactly why.

They were all sitting around a wooden table, Blaze at the center, Kareem at the right side and Marq on the left. Kareem had the biggest grin on his face, as Anika stared at him angrily and Marquise couldn't help but chuckle.

"Yo... You got a loyal, brave trap queen over here B'," Kareem said. Blaze said nothing and just smiled happily as he got up out his seat.

"Baby, yo-"

"What the fuck's going on Blaze?!" she questioned him furiously, watching him walk towards her. "You left me alone out there! And then I see four guys, with machetes and guns enter in here!"

So she's brave and got a mouth on her? I like her already, Marquise mused happily watching the way she shouted at Blaze.

"Anika, let m-"

"What kind of sick game are you playing with me Malik?! I almost risk my life to check up on you and here you are playing fucking cards with your boys!" she exclaimed, interrupting him, fired up and infuriated with him.

Blaze paused momentarily before asking, "Yo' ass done shoutin' now?"

"Yes," she mumbled sulkily.

"I didn't know about what just happened until I came in here. Kareem," Blaze said as he turned and pointed Kareem, "was the one who planned this shit with Marquise, behind my back."

Anika looked at the boys, still annoyed. Marquise and Kareem continued grinning at her and watching her carefully. She was beautiful. Marquise couldn't deny it even if he tried. He could definitely see why Blaze was hooked on her and now, crazy about her. Mama had a body on her, slim, curvy hips with a nice shaped butt.

"They said they wanted to meet you, but they ain't say when exactly. So imagine my surprise when I turn up here, thinkin' we have an emergency but they planned this shit to test you, to see if you were really down for me. And now I can see that you are baby," Blaze concluded lovingly.

"Yeah Anika, you the realest and baddest trap queen Blaze ever had," Kareem commented.

"And you ain't no punk," Marquise stated boldly with a smirk. "I like that shit."

Looking at the way Blaze was so passionate and loving with his girl, made Marquise begin thinking of Nicole. Nicole. His baby. He missed her and hoped to see her really soon. She was now his everything and he would make sure that he spent the rest of his days making her happy.

He began searching in his front pocket for his iPhone and when he found it, he went straight to his text messages to text his baby and see if she was down for meeting up with him tonight. It was only when he began to type that a text notification from Masika chimed in.

"Have you talked to him yet for me?"
Marquise: *"Not yet, been busy."*
Masika: *"Please make it quick. U my only hope."*
Marquise: *"Yeah I'll talk to him soon."*
Masika: *"Call me when you do."*

Now seeing his boy so happy with Anika made Marquise realize that talking to Blaze about Masika was probably never going to happen. He needed to figure out a way to officially cut Masika off too, because she was becoming annoying as fuck. Anika was one bad trap queen and a perfect fit for Blaze.

Fuck Masika.

***

"Baby can I see u tonite?"

Naomi smiled down at the latest text message from Marquise and quickly typed back, *"I'll let u know."*

"Naomi, best believe your husband contacted me wanting me to talk to you about your 'marriage'," Erin announced with a smirk.

"Really?" Naomi put her phone down and focused on listening to what her best friend suddenly had to say. "When?"

"A few days ago," she stated simply. "He wouldn't stop going on and on about how you've been treating him."

"Do you think I'm a horrible person?" Naomi asked, genuinely wanting to know the honest answer from her friend.

"No hun," Erin said. "Just a person who was fed up of having shitty dick all the time and a nigga that did nothing for his family."

"I do feel bad though," Naomi admitted. "I've been treating him so bad, he could up and leave me anytime."

"Isn't that what you want?"

"Marquise doesn't really seem down for marriage or kids," Naomi responded. "I gotta look out for my kids. Tyree's the only father they'll ever have."

"So stop treating him so bad," Erin advised. "If you don't want him to leave you, then still be good to him and still have Marquise all to yourself."

"So I be civil with him?"

"Yeah, just be civil. You ain't gotta force yourself to sleep with him. You don't need dick, you got Marquise's bomb ass one already. Just be civil with your husband; he can be the side dude and Marquise can be the main."

***

Naomi decided to take her best friend's advice and sit down with her husband and sort things out. It was better for them to be civil, than for them to be constantly biting each other's heads off.

Naomi waited patiently for Tyree to walk back into their shared bedroom and when he did with a neutral facial expression, she called out to him.

"Tyree."

"Yes?"

"We need to talk," she voiced gently.

"About?" he queried with an arched brow.

"Us."

"Oh, so now you want to talk about us? What happened to not giving a fuck?" he rudely questioned.

"Please come and sit down Tyree. I'm not trying to argue with you tonight, I just want us to sort things out."

So he did as she asked, sitting down next to her and listening to what she had to say. Naomi tried to put on the best act she could play and tell Tyree how good of a father he was to their kids and for that, she would forever love him. She just wanted them to be good again and end all the arguments and fights. All she wanted was peace.

Tyree agreed to peace and told her how much he loved her and just wanted his wife back. When Naomi kept silent at his words and looked away, guilty, he decided to take matters into his own hands.

"Tyree, what... what are you doing?"

It had been a minute since he had had sex with his wife. He missed being intimate with her and taking her to places that he knew only he could. He was sure that she had missed being with him as much as he had.

"What does it look like I'm doin' babe?" he questioned her sexily.

"It... It looks like you're getting naked... for me."

And he was doing exactly just that because in the next five minutes, he was completely butt ass naked in front of her. Her heart began to race with pure lust and excitement as she looked at his long, length that was automatically calling her name.

"I am sweetheart," he voiced happily with a sexy smirk now plastered upon his handsome face. "I've missed you, ain't you missed me?"

Naomi couldn't lie. Looking at her husband's sexy body had her sweating and heating up with excitement. When was the last time that she had examined her husband's fine ass body? He wasn't as big as Marquise when it came to the muscle department but when it came to dick length, Tyree seemed a little bigger. Nah... Maybe she was dreaming. Marquise was definitely the bigger candidate.

Within the next five minutes, Naomi was suddenly completely naked for him and ready for whatever he had planned as he made her kneel frontwards on their bed. Her butt poking out towards him.

"Shit," she suddenly groaned, feeling him slowly push his thick length inside her, completely filling her up with his big dick.

"Oooo...Ty." Her moans just couldn't be concealed, and once he started moving, neither could his.

In and out he pounded inside her, watching her take it all. Her ass jiggled as he eased in and out of her, his deep thrusts and strokes getting faster by the minute.

"Yes baby...fuck me!" She felt so good around his shaft - tight, firm, and getting wetter by the second. "Harder Ty...fuck yes..."

"God damn...this how you want it, baby?" he groaned deeply, pulling his dick back out and quickly pushing it back in again. Her legs shook as he pushed into her, slamming their bodies together and watching that fat ass of hers that he loved so much jiggle back and forth.

The hard smacking noise of their bodies colliding together, moans, and groans echoed in the bedroom. "You better twerk your sexy ass on this dick babe...yeah...just like that."

He tightened his hold on her hips, watching as her ass moved. He kept rapidly rocking her body hard, back and forward on his dick.

He groaned deep with each thrust, roughly massaging his hands against her hot skin. With each fast pump of his hips, Ty felt like he was going to lose control and burst.

Then he pushed her face down towards the bed, so that her face was squashed against their red pillows. Naomi wasn't expecting Tyree to be so rough with her. He was never rough. But with her face down and her ass up, she was loving every single minute of it.

He softly sighed, nudging the soft seal of her pussy before slowly pushing his tip inside of her tight hole. His fingers found their way to hold onto her sides for support as he pushed his tip further into her pussy. She was so tight for him. Tight, wet, and firm.

"Shit, Ty..." she gently moaned immediately, turning him on even more. He tightened his fingers around her sides, pushing his length between her slick folds, penetrating deeper inside her.

"Fuck," he groaned and rocked his hips into her firm ass, the bed dipping under the shifting weight of their bodies as he thrust his dick inside her soaked pussy to a steady rhythm. The more she moaned, the quicker he filled her up with his dick.

Every hard inch of his dick was buried deep between her legs. He spread her legs a little further, allowing her to adjust to his dick, filling her fully. She moaned softly when he started rocking back and forth, allowing her to feel each hard ridge and curve of his thickness.

"Ty...that feels so... damn good," she groaned, tilting her pelvis a little higher so he could push deeper into her pussy.

He dug his fingertips deeper into her sides, forcefully pulling her hips back against his. "Fuck, Naomi...baby," he groaned. The harder and faster he drove into her, the better it felt. He reached underneath her, wrapping his fingers around her bouncing breasts, leaning into her back more. "So nice and tight..." he groaned, squeezing her hard nipples between his fingers.

He started increasing the force and speed in his thrusts, jerking her body harder against his. Her firm ass cheeks collided roughly against his pelvis, creaking the bed springs underneath them. He groaned deep in his throat with each pull of his dick out her pussy.

His lips found their way onto her neck, kissing and sucking at her warm, soft flesh. Then before she knew it, he flipped her around so that she was facing him this time and he could easily fit in between her legs.

Then he began.

"Ty...don't stop...please..." The bed violently creaked underneath them, the headboard roughly rocking against the wall as he increased the speed of his smooth thrusts. She almost screamed out in pleasure as he pushed faster, moving her hands from his sides, to hold on to his back.

"Bomb ass pussy," he whispered sexily into her ear, still thrusting into her.

She buried her face against his neck, sucking and kissing at his hot skin. The only thing that could be heard right now was her moans, his groans, their skin slapping together, and the bed rocking and creaking. She moaned louder, rocking her hips faster and harder. She was very close.

He moved his hands to rest on her hips, pumping himself between her legs faster and harder according to her loud moans. "Fuck... Naomi!" he groaned, pulling her hips tightly against his.

"Ty...shit, I'm gonna cum... uhh!" she gasped loudly. Her heart quickly raced and her breaths came out quicker and shorter. Her hands reached for his neck, cupping her fingers tightly around his chocolate skin.

"Ugh...Uhhh!" Her fingertips pressed firmly into his neck, holding him tighter as she pumped her hips up and down. Her body began to tense in his arms. "Ty!" she cried out as her body froze underneath him. Her climax rushed hot and fast to his thick dick, covering every inch.

"Fuck baby," he groaned loudly, thrusting hard inside of her one last time before he burst inside of her.

CHAPTER 18 ~ OLD FLAME

While Tyree hopped into their en-suite shower, Naomi lay naked in ecstasy at the hot events that had just occurred between them. She was so sore. So sore and her warm, wet thighs were still shaking. This nigga had just put it down on her and left like nothing had happened! As if he had not just fucked her brains out and almost broken their damn bed.

She couldn't believe it. Who was this man and what had he done with her husband? She stared at the ceiling as the flashbacks of what she'd just experienced played over and over in her head. She felt the butterflies swarming in her stomach which was unusual for her. Lately, Marq had been the one to bring those feelings out of her, but at that very moment, Marq was the furthest thing from her mind. She closed her eyes and exhaled while trying to relax her body which was still shaking from their session.

She was exhausted from their previous session and the only thing she wanted was a hot shower at the moment. She decided she would just lay there until Tyree had finished. Before she knew it, Naomi drifted off to sleep and was awakened by Tyree whispering in her ear.

"Hey, I gotta run out for a minute. Do you want anything before I go?"

Naomi instantly sat up in bed and squinted as her eyes tried to adjust to the room. She stared at her husband and the sight of him turned her on. She bit down on her bottom lip as she attempted to gather her thoughts.

"Where are you going?" Naomi questioned.

Tyree smiled as he moved towards her. He kissed her on the forehead and replied "I won't be long babe. Gotta meet up with the guys for a few drinks."

Naomi smirked slightly and replied, "Okay. What time will the kids be back?"

"They'll be gone for a few more hours," Tyree said as he walked out of the bedroom. "See you later beautiful."

"Okay! See you later," Naomi yelled after him. She slid out of bed just as she heard the front door close behind him. She glanced at the clock on the nightstand and realized she'd been sleep for a whole hour. She stretched her arms over her head and smiled at the ache between her legs. She walked to their en-suite and turned on the shower, allowing the steam to fill the room. She couldn't wait to stand under the steaming hot shower and allow it to provide some relief to her stiff body.

***

Naomi sat in the living room while attempting to read a book. With both Tyree and the kids gone, the house was too quiet. Filling the void with a book until they all came home was the easiest thing that came to mind, but she was having a hard time focusing. Her mind kept going back to how good Tyree had put it on her earlier. She never thought he had it in him considering he had always been such a gentle lover. Hell, she hadn't even realized what she'd been missing until she met Marquise.

Naomi grabbed her phone off of the end table and decided to call Erin for some girl talk. She needed to clear her head and she was the only person she could talk to about her love triangle. She quickly dialed Erin to tell her everything.

"Hello?" Erin answered.

"Hey girl. You busy?" Naomi questioned.

"Nah. I was just cleaning up, but I can take a break," Erin replied.

"I got something to tell you Erin and I need your honest opinion," Naomi confided.

"Okay, spill bitch! You know you the only one getting some action and I love living vicariously through you," Erin laughed as she flopped down onto her sofa.

"Whateva bitch, please! You got way more options than me and last time I checked, you had a date last night," Naomi teased.

"Yeah, a boring suit who wouldn't know how to hit this pussy right even if I handed him a manual," Erin exclaimed.

They both burst into laughter at the thought of it all. Naomi shook her head knowing that her best friend was dead serious. Erin didn't play when it came to her boy toys and if they couldn't handle her, they were gone with the quickness.

"Come on Erin! I need your advice and I don't have a lot of time to talk about this before Tyree and the kids get home," Naomi whined.

"Okay, okay. Now what happened bitch and don't leave out any details!" Erin demanded.

Naomi went on to tell her best friend everything that had taken place earlier during the day and of course, she spared no details.

"Wait, so Ty put it down?" Erin asked in a confused tone.

"Yes girl," Naomi admitted.

"We talkin' about the same Ty right? You ain't go find a new nigga did you?" Erin laughed.

"Hey, I resent that! Besides, I'm already having a hard enough time juggling two niggas, let alone a third," Naomi admitted.

"So how does all this make you feel?" Erin giggled.

"To be honest Erin, I didn't really realize until today that somewhere along the way I lost myself and I have to get that girl back," Naomi admitted.

"What do you mean?" Erin questioned.

"Well for one, I could be spending way more time with my kids and doing things with them just like I used to. You know, cooking for them, going to the park, and just playing with them. All of the things I used to do before," Naomi declared.

"You mean before you met Marquise?" Erin asked.

"Yeah," Naomi admitted.

"Are you blaming this change in you on Marquise?" Erin asked.

"No, of course not! I'm woman enough to say that all of this is my fault. Not to mention the fact that he knows nothing about my kids and told me he's not sure about children right now. I just don't know how I let all of this spiral out of control," Naomi admitted.

"I hear ya girl, but what's done is done so don't beat yourself up about it. Besides, you really don't know if Marquise is being 100% honest with you himself. I mean we both know how these niggas are and that's why I always told you to do you. You come to a decision when you're good and ready. When you know you'll know," Erin exclaimed.

Naomi smiled at her best friend's words. She truly appreciated the fact that she could vent to her without ever being judged or looked down upon. A lesser woman would have probably turned up their nose at the things that Naomi had been doing lately, but not Erin. She proved time and time again that she had her back. For that Naomi was grateful.

"Thanks so much for the girl talk Erin. You're amazing," Naomi smiled.

"No problem girl," Erin stated.

"Well, I'll let you get back to cleaning your pig sty," Naomi laughed.

"Hey now bitch, watch yo'self. I don't live in a pig sty alright? It's more like a pig pen so get it right," Erin declared as the both burst into laughter. They said their goodbyes and Naomi placed her phone on the end table next to the chair she was sitting in, just as the front door flew open.

"Mommy! Mommy!" her daughter yelled as she ran through the front door along with her brother and Tyree.

Naomi stretched her arms and wrapped them around both of her children. "Hey babies! Mommy missed you guy so much!" Naomi said sweetly.

She glanced towards Tyree who was smiling from ear to ear at the sight of it all. She returned the smile and immediately felt a warmth inside of her that she hadn't felt for some time now.

"So how about we all go and make dinner together," Tyree said as he glanced in his wife's direction.

Naomi smiled at the gesture. She knew Tyree was trying his hardest to make up with her and to keep the positive vibes flowing. "Yes, let's make dinner together as a family," she said.

The kids ran off to the kitchen and Tyree followed behind them. Naomi stood up and noticed that her cell phone was vibrating on the table next to her. She quickly grabbed it and opened the text that just came through.

Marq: *"Nic I miss u n I need you in my bed 2 nite."*

Naomi: *"Sorry I can't. I'm really busy tonight."*

Naomi exhaled as she thought about what she'd just done.

"Are you coming?" Tyree asked as he peeked around the corner from the other room.

"Yes," Naomi smiled as she tucked her phone in her pocket and made her way towards the kitchen. She was determined to enjoy her night with the family without the thought of Marquise crossing her mind.

***

Naomi sat at the kitchen table while sorting through her graded papers. She'd come straight home after work because she'd fallen so behind with grading her papers. As she sat at the kitchen table, she flinched as the familiar sound of a text alert filled the room. She was home alone at the time, but knew her family would be walking through the door at any moment now. Tyree had taken them both to the park, allowing Naomi some time to get caught up on her work.

Naomi reached for her phone and slowly read the text.

Marq: *"Baby am I gonna see you tonite?"*

Naomi hesitated before responding. She chewed her bottom lip and said

Naomi: *"Sorry not tonight. I have so much work to get caught up on."*

Naomi went back to her papers as she waited for a response from Marquise. She felt butterflies swarming inside of her because she knew that how much he hated to hear the word no.

Marq: *"Nic? I miss you so much and I know you miss me too."*

Naomi: *"I know and of course I do. I'm so sorry."*

Marq: *"Look Nic idk whats going on but, I betta see yo ass soon girl."*

Naomi: *"Marq I just told you what's going on. I'm busy with work."*

Marq: *"Sounds like BS, but if you say so."*

Naomi rolled her eyes at Marquise's response. She knew all too well how much of a brat he could be when he didn't get his way.

Naomi: *"I'll see you soon Marq ok? But right now I have to grade papers. Talk to u later."*

Marq: *"Whateva ma."*

Naomi exhaled and sat the phone down. She didn't expect their conversation to go to the left so quickly. Just when she thought she was done, another text came through.

Marq: *"I love you Nic. Don't eva forget that."*

Naomi: *"Stop Marq, and I love you too."*

Naomi shook her head as she exited her texts and set her phone down once again. *What in the hell was that all about? Does Marq know something?* Before she had a chance to fully think things through, she could hear Tyree putting his key in the door. She immediately grabbed her cell and placed it on silent just in case Marq decided to text her again.

Tyree walked through the front door alone and immediately Naomi was turned on by the sight of him.

"Where are the kids?" Naomi asked as she continued to eye his muscles through his shirt.

"I forgot to tell you that I enrolled them in Girl and Boy Scouts last week. Today was a field trip so they won't be back for a few hours," Tyree explained as he began walking into the kitchen.

Naomi watched him intently as he came and stood directly next to her. She started gathering her papers that she'd graded and placing them neatly inside of the bins she'd created.

"You finished?" Tyree asked.

"Yeah. I was going to get started on dinner, but since the kids are gone I don't know if I should start just yet," Naomi concluded.

"Or maybe you should let me have you for dinner," Tyree boldly declared as he gently swept a strand of hair from her face before tucking it behind her ear.

Naomi's stomach did summersaults from his touch. She inhaled his musky scent and instantly became wet. The new Tyree was turning her on in a major way and she loved every moment of it. Tyree pulled her chair back and Naomi stood up moving out from under the table. Tyree walked up behind her and took her ear into his mouth. He licked, sucked, and nibbled on her ear lobe, sending chills down her spine before moving to her neck. Naomi's soft moans filled the kitchen while his hands explored her curves.

Tyree moved his hand to her pussy and in one swift move, he began rubbing her throbbing clit.

"Look how wet my pussy is," Tyree moaned into her ear.

Naomi's head fell back on his shoulder as she turned slightly so their lips could meet. She sucked his tongue while his other hand squeezed her breasts.

"Tyree," Naomi moaned gently, enjoying the feel of his manly hands squeezing her tits.

Tyree then lifted the bottom of the dress she was wearing, up over her hip sand ripped her panties from her body.

"Ah," Naomi moaned as pushed her forward until her breasts were touching the cold wooden table.

Tyree smacked her ass hard and said "Tell me you want this dick Naomi!"

"Ah! I want you now!" Naomi moaned as loud as she possibly could. She was raining wet and ready for her husband to push his way inside her.

Before she knew it, Ty's dick was on her clit causing Naomi's legs to begin to shake.

"Please," Naomi begged.

"Please what Naomi?" Tyree said as he began to rub small circles around her entrance with the tip of his hard dick.

"Please fuck me now! I need you, daddy," Naomi moaned.

Tyree wasted no time as he plunged inside of her while grabbing a handful of her hair. He pounded in and out of her as the sound of her ass slapping against him filled the room.

"Yes daddy! That's right, fuck me!" Naomi yelled.

"Fuck, you feel good!" Tyree moaned as he began to pound faster and faster. He smacked her on the ass causing Naomi to yell out in pleasure.

"Oh my God!" she screamed as Tyree began rubbing her clit with his free hand.

"That's right baby, cum all on this dick," Tyree moaned while Naomi began throwing her ass back harder than before. Naomi knew for sure that Tyree was one beast in the sheets and out them too.

"Yes! Yes! I'm about to cum!" Naomi screamed.

Tyree began to pound harder and harder while firmly gripping her shoulders.

"Ah! Tyree!" Naomi screamed as her hot juices seeped out of her. Her orgasm crashed over her body in a wave so powerful she was sure she was going blind. Tyree continued to pound in and out of her until he too felt his wave approaching.

"Fuck, this pussy so good!" Tyree yelled as he came inside of her.

They both leaned against the table for support as they attempted to catch their breath. Naomi was completely spent as his head rested on her back between her shoulder blades. Tyree had once again put it down, leaving her completely in shock.

"So you still gonna cook or nah?" Tyree asked as they both began to laugh.

Normally she would have been too tired, but not today. Today he could have whatever he wanted.

CHAPTER 19 ~ CHOOSING RIGHT

Marquise: *"Nah, lover boy's too preoccupied waiting for his girl to come out with us right now Kareem."*

Kareem: *"I know... The boy's been feening for the pussy all week."*

Marquise stared down at his bright screen and couldn't help but laugh at his group chat with his boys. He and Kareem were currently teasing Blaze about how whipped he was because of how much he was feeling and missing Anika. Marquise knew she meant everything to him now.

Blaze: *"Chill... I've missed her."*

Kareem: *"We kno' you've missed her..."*

Marquise: *"And that pussy too!"*

Marquise couldn't lie. He missed Nicole. He hadn't seen her in like forever it seemed. He needed to see her soon or else he felt he was going to lose his damn mind.

Blaze: *"Any word on Leek?"*

Kareem: *"Nah... Still searchin'."*

Marquise: *"Since when did that nigga become so good at runnin'?"*

Blaze: *"Don't worry, we gon' get his ass. He can run but he can't hide."*

Kareem: *"Bet."*

Blaze: *"I'm out. Bonnie's here."*

Bonnie was the nickname Marq and Kareem had both given Anika once she had passed their test. Blaze seemed to like it too, so ever since then that's what they had been calling her.

Bonnie.

Marquise liked the fact that Anika was down for Blaze. She was brave and determined, not to forget fucking gorgeous. All Marq wanted was his own Bonnie too. He was praying that it was Nicole. He was falling for her deeply and was willing to change up his whole act for her. If she wanted kids, he was down. If she wanted marriage, he was down too. All he wanted was her.

With that being said, Marquise quickly went to Nicole's number and called her line. When she didn't pick up the first time, he tried again. And when she didn't pick up the second time, he still kept trying.

"What the fuck you playin' at ma?" he asked angrily as he listened to the dial tone of his phone.

***

It had been weeks since she'd seen Marquise. Naomi had been dodging his calls and often sent him to voicemail. She had been making excuses as to why she couldn't see him and now he was calling nonstop. Naomi rolled her eyes as she declined his call for the fourth time today. She decided to turn her phone off completely since Tyree and the kids were home. They'd been getting along pretty well and she didn't want to go back down the same road again.

Naomi smiled as Tyree entered the room. He'd just fucked her brains out once again and they'd gotten pretty loud which resulted in their son waking up. Tyree had just put him back to bed and came to lay back down beside her. She turned to face him as they laid quietly while staring at each other.

"What happened to us babe?" Tyree asked.

"Life," Naomi responded.

"But when did you become so unhappy? When did you fall out of love with me?" Tyree questioned while staring into her eyes.

Naomi felt like shit. It was as if her heart had just broken in two as those words fell from his lips.

"Baby, I never ever stopped loving you," Naomi admitted.

"Look, I know we've been through a lot these last few months. I just don't understand how or when shit got so bad between us. I don't know how I lost my best friend," Tyree declared.

"I'm still here Tyree, and I know things got pretty bad, but we can fix this. I'm not the only one who said some pretty harsh things," Naomi declared.

"I know and I was out of line, Naomi. But just talking about this right now is not going to fix this," Tyree declares.

Naomi knew exactly what he was getting at. Tyree had suggested counselling before and he was throwing it out there again. When she'd said no before, she was so wrapped up in Marq that she really didn't care about what he'd wanted her to do. But, she knew that if she wanted her family to stay together, counselling was the only answer to getting their marriage back on track.

"I'll do it," Naomi stated.

Tyree smiled. "Really? You'll go to counselling with me so that we can get over our issues?"

"Yes I will, but if a nigga tries to play that damn Doctor Phil card, I'm out!" Naomi laughed as Tyree pulled her closer. He gently kissed her lips and held her in his arms.

"I love you so much," he stated.

"I love you more," Naomi declared.

It had been such a long time since she'd said those words to her husband, let alone spent some quality time with him. Now that things had gotten better between the two of them, she had to admit that there was no other place she'd rather be.

***

The next morning, a frantic Tyree woke Naomi from her sleep to share some good news with her. He'd gotten a job working nights at a 24-hour gym and he just couldn't wait to tell her. Naomi was ecstatic that her husband had not only found employment, but that he had a new glow about him. In that moment she realized that her husband had lost himself as well. They'd both been so consumed with everyday life that they forgot to stop and smell the roses every once in a while. Naomi promised herself from here on out, that she would make sure they did just that.

Shortly afterwards, Tyree insisted they go on a family outing as a celebration of their new income. They went out to eat at their favorite restaurant and while eating, Ty promised to hit every store imaginable for his family tomorrow. They were going to go out on a long shopping trip to the mall.

Tyree was so happy that he was splurging big time on her and the kids. Naomi truly enjoyed her husband and never once had she thought of Marq. By the grace of God, he hadn't called all day which left her in a great mood.

After Tyree ran out to drop some paperwork off to his new job location and the kids were outside playing in the backyard, Naomi decided she should share the exciting news with her bestie. She dialed Erin and of course she picked up after the first ring.

"Hey bitch! You betta have some good tea to spill," Erin declared.

Naomi chuckled, "Well don't I always?"

"Yeah you do, so spill now bitch! I'm dying over here," Erin laughed.

"Okay, well for one things have been so great between me and Tyree. My God the sex has been consistently amazing and we've been getting along so well, you know?" Naomi said.

"Okay, and what about Marq? Have you talked to him or seen him?" Erin questioned.

"I haven't seen him since I started back sleeping with Tyree. I barely talk to him anymore because I'm always with my family now," Naomi admitted.

"Okay, and how are you gonna manage that?" Erin asked.

"What do you mean?" Naomi responded. She was totally thrown off by Erin's tone at the moment. The once cheery and bubbly personality she normally displayed was replaced with a negative tone. Naomi was offended by it.

"I mean I told you to play nice, not fuck up what you got with Marq. Look, I know things seem all good and dandy between you and hubby right now, but Tyree will get back to the same old boring shit after a while, trust me. What you need to do is keep ya' boo on the side because that's where the real is," Erin declared.

Naomi stopped in mid stride as she took in all that Erin had just said.

"I don't know about all that Erin, but what I do know is Tyree is a real man. He always has been and always will be in my book. Funny how you never seemed to have a problem with him before I met Marq," Naomi stated.

"Come on now, Naomi. Wake up and open your eyes, okay? What real man allows his wife to solely take care of his household while he stays at home with the kids like some damn nanny? Tyree has never been the man of the house per say, but I never said anything because you're my best friend and it wasn't my place," Erin concluded.

"Well for your information, my man has a job now and is taking care of his family just fine. You are right about one thing though; it's not your place so keep your opinion about my man to yourself. As a matter of a fact, I need to go because this conversation has definitely taken a different turn," Naomi stated rudely.

"Look, I'm not trying to judge you Naomi. You know I love you and I'll support you through whateva, but I won't lie to you to protect your feelings. I think you really need to think this through before you go running back to your husband. Sure Marq may have some things to work on, but who doesn't? Think on it okay and make sure you make the right decision so you won't regret it later," Erin exclaimed.

"Yeah I hear you. Gotta go, talk to you later," Naomi said as she hung up the phone before giving Erin a chance to respond.

She never knew that her friend disliked her husband so much, but she definitely knew now. She decided that there was no more listening to or confiding in Erin. She was right about one thing though, Naomi did need to choose and she did. She was choosing her husband and kids. Naomi was choosing her family over lust and she was positive that she was making the right decision.

Naomi scrolled through her contacts until she found Marq's number. She stared at the number for a moment before saying *"It was good while it lasted. Goodbye Marq."*

Naomi added Marq to the blocked list until she got the chance to change her number. Right now she wanted to make sure her family had dinner on the table. Afterwards, her hubby would have her for desert.

CHAPTER 20 ~ CAUGHT

Marquise: *"Baby, I need to see u."*

Marquise: *"Nic, you there?"*

Marquise: *"Why u always busy?"*

Marquise: *"I miss u... and that pussy too."*

Marquise: *"I need to see u real soon. I don't give a fuck 'bout yo' damn job no more. I haven't seen u for almost a month now."*

Marquise: *"My dick misses u."*

Marquise didn't understand what was taking Nicole so long to reply to his messages. But then when he got the text notification at 8pm telling him that she had finally replied, he was smiling ear to ear. His smile quickly disappeared once he read her message though.

"It was good while it lasted. Goodbye Marq."

What the fuck? What was up with her? Marquise's anger only continued to build once he dialed her number but was sent straight to voicemail. He didn't even get to hear the line dial or anything, it just went straight to voicemail, which only pissed him off further.

"This bitch didn't jus' block my number," he snapped angrily, still trying to get through to her. But seeing that he wasn't getting anywhere, Marquise stopped trying.

What the hell did she mean that it was good while it lasted? Marquise was praying that she wasn't thinking of ending things between them. He didn't want to end things with her. Not when he was deep in love with her.

He figured that she was probably just getting a bit emotional and it was probably her time of the month again. He would give her some space and hope that she came back to him.

~ The Next Day ~

"Nah, I ain't spoken to him yet," Marquise stated simply. "We been busy Mas. You kno' what we do."

"I know… But do you think you could speed up the process please?"

Masika was just becoming more and more annoying, the more that Marquise was forced to stay on the phone with her. He wasn't planning to ever speak to Blaze about their relationship. Blaze was happily in love with another chick. Masika was just gonna have to get over it.

"Look Masika, I ain't got time for this bullshit anymore. Blaze doesn't want you anymore. He's with someone else. So you jus' gon' have to get used to that. I'm sorry but that's just the way things are at the moment."

"But you said you were gonna he-"

Marquise suddenly cut over her, "Move on Masika. He's done with you," he concluded before hanging up the phone.

Today he had bigger fish to fry than to worry about Masika's stupid clingy ass. He told himself that he was going to stay away from Nicole, but there was nothing wrong with him treating her from afar.

He knew that if he bought her some sexy designer shit and sent it to her workplace, she would come running back in no time.

So that's exactly what he planned to do.

***

"Mmm… Ty, we gotta go, the kids are waiting," Naomi whispered softly, enjoying Tyree's neck kisses and his hands moving up her waist to her breasts.

The moment he squeezed both in his warm palms, she swore she was losing all control over her body. But they needed to go.

"Ty…"

"Just a quickie baby," he responded sexily. "With the way your ass been movin' in that sundress… I need to get some now."

Naomi giggled lightly at his comment before turning around to face her husband's handsome face. "But daddy, I don't want a quickie right now."

"You don't?"

She shook her head no before responding, "I want a long lovemaking session when we get back from the mall."

"But baby, I'm so damn horny right now," he begged. "Let me get some now and I'll give you so-"

"Dad! Mom! Can we go now?" Josie called out to her parents from their living room, ready to go to the mall.

"We're coming darlings!" Naomi responded happily, before planting a sweet kiss on Ty's lips and pulling him out their bedroom.

"You lucky we gotta go," Tyree said. "Cause when we come back that ass is all mine."

"Okay daddy," Naomi replied shyly.

Ten minutes later, The Evans were happily riding in their family car heading to the mall. While Tyree drove, Naomi couldn't help but reminisce on Marq. She hoped he was okay. She did regret ending their relationship like that, but she had to do what she had to do. There was no way that she could handle being with two dudes at the same time. It wouldn't work. One would find out and that would be the end of everything. It was best she just chose the man that she had been with from the start - her husband.

When finally making it to the mall, Christopher and Josie were extremely excited.

"Mommy, I wanna go to the clothing store!" Josie shouted happily.

"Dad, I wanna go to sports store!" Christopher demanded.

So Tyree and Naomi knew the only way to make everyone happy was if they split up and went to the different stores that their kids wanted to go to.

"We'll be in H&M, so when you guys are done you can come meet us then we'll go get a bite to eat," Naomi explained.

ADDICTED TO MY THUG

"Alright baby. See you in a bit," Tyree concluded, giving her a quick peck and waving to Josie before leading an excited Chris to the sports store. Naomi knew how much her son loved playing sports, especially basketball. She was just hoping that Tyree didn't buy him another ball; he had way too many of those already.

"Alright sweetie, you ready to get some new clothes?"

"Yeah Mom," Josie said before running off into the store.

"Slow down babe, you know mama's not as young as she used to be," Naomi laughingly stated before quickly following in after her energetic daughter.

When they started browsing some tops and skirts together, Naomi couldn't help but notice how happy she was that she was spending some quality time with her daughter. Times like these were times she cherished the most. Just talking to her nine-year-old about school, staying well away from boys and cracking jokes with her. She lived for moments like these.

"Josie what'd you think of this shirt. It's cute right?... Josie, what do you... Josie?" Naomi turned around only to see Josie running off to where she could see shoes in her size.
Naomi quickly followed and helped her pick out the cutest shoes in her size. Once they were done paying for all of Josie's things, using Tyree's new credit card, they were heading out ready to meet up with Tyree and Christopher.

However, seeing the flashy Louis Vuitton store ahead was now calling Naomi's name to enter inside. She sent Ty a quick text before heading inside with Josie.

While Josie ran off, Naomi was automatically distracted by the pretty bags laid out on display and now calling her name. The second she picked one up, she knew she wanted it. It suited her so well and while modelling it in the store mirror, she knew she just had to have it.

"Josie, what do you think of..." It was only when she remembered that Josie had run off somewhere in the store that she realized her daughter couldn't say her opinions on the bag.

So she put the bag back in its place and went deeper into the store looking for her daughter.

"Josie! Josie where are you?" She didn't care that people in the store were giving her crazy looks as she called out to Josie. She was a mother and her daughter's wellbeing always came first.

However, when she finally found Josie, Naomi stopped frozen in her tracks, unable to move on.

Josie was sitting on the customer chairs, trying on a pair of Louis Vuitton flats. But it wasn't the trying on of the shoes that had her shook, it was the stranger helping her try on the shoes.

Marquise.

"Mom, don't these look pretty on me?" Josie looked up at her mother with a grin. "My new friend, Marquise helped me pick them out."

Marquise turned around to see who his new little friend's mom was. He wasn't even going to help the young girl at first, but with the way she was struggling to reach the shoes she wanted, he felt bad for her.

He almost had to do a double take once he saw Nicole standing, watching him.

"Nicole?!"

Naomi didn't know what to do or say, she just kept still and silent. She was hoping this was a nightmare. A nightmare she could wake up from any second now.

But she didn't wake up. Instead, things took a slight turn for the worse once Tyree and Christopher had arrived at the store.

Christopher ran to his sister and looked down at her shoes with disgust. "Those are ugly on you."

"Hey, don't be so mean to your sister Chris," Tyree ordered firmly before moving towards his wife. He gave her a sweet kiss on her cheek before asking, "Baby, is everything okay?" He sensed her strange mood and noticed the strange man standing in front of Josie while she tried on her designer shoes.

All Naomi could do was stare ahead straight into Marquise's hazel eyes, with shock at what was happening. She wanted to cry. No… She wanted to die.

"So, Naomi is it?" Marquise rudely questioned her.

"Yeah, she's my wife. Problem bro?" Tyree asked boldly, not liking the way this man was talking and looking at Naomi.

"Problem?" Marquise responded with a cold look to Naomi. "Yeah man, there's a serious fuckin' problem."

All Naomi could do was stare at Tyree and then back at Marquise. Her husband and her lover now in the same environment. And there was nowhere to run or hide.

What the hell was she going to do?

~ To Be Continued ~

~ *Thank From Ari & Miss Jen* ~

Thank you so much for reading Ari & Miss Jenesequa's novel.

Please *do not forget to drop a review on Amazon, it will be greatly appreciated and we would love to hear what you thought about this novel! Don't forget to check out Ari's other works:*

- *I'll Ride For My Thug 1 & 2 & 3*
- *Love, Betrayal & Dirty Money: A Hood Romance*
  - *Feel free to connect with Ari at:*
  https://www.facebook.com/Author Ari

- *And Miss Jenesequa's other works:*
  - *Lustful Desires: Secrets, Sex & Lies*
  - *Sex Ain't Better Than Love 1 & 2*
  - *Luvin' Your Man: Tales Of A Side Chick*
  - *Down For My Baller 1 & 2*
  - *Bad For My Thug 1 & 2*

- *Feel free to connect with Miss Jenesequa at:*
  https://www.facebook.com/AuthorMissJenesequa
  www.missjenesequa.com

Please make sure to leave a review! We love reading them. Thank you so much for the support and love. We really do appreciate it.

Ari

Miss Jenesequa

Looking for a publishing home?
Royalty Publishing House, Where the Royals reside, is accepting submissions for writers in the urban fiction genre. If you're interested, submit the first 3-4 chapters with your synopsis to submissions@royaltypublishinghouse.com. Check out our website for more information: www.royaltypublishinghouse.com.

Be sure to LIKE our Royalty Publishing House page on Facebook

CPSIA information can be obtained at www.ICGtesting.com
Printed in the USA
LVOW10s1807160916

504963LV00017B/212/P